ANYONE BUT YOU

CHELSEA M. CAMERON

Get Free Books!

Tropetastic romance with a twist, Happily Ever Afters guaranteed! You can expect humor and heart in every Chelsea M. Cameron romance.

Get a free book today! Join Chelsea's Newsletter and get a copy of Marriage of Unconvenience, about two best friends who get fake married to share an inheritance and end up with a lot of *real* feelings.

And now, back to Anyone But You…

About Anyone but You

Things are going great for Sutton Kay, or at least they were. Her yoga studio is doing well, she's living with her best friend, and she just got two kittens named Mocha and Cappuccino. Sure, she doesn't have a girlfriend, but her life is full and busy.

Then her building is sold and the new landlord turns out to be the woman putting in a gym downstairs who doesn't seem to understand the concepts "courtesy" and "don't be rude to your tenants." Sutton can't get a read on Tuesday Grímsdóttir, but she can appreciate her muscles. Seriously, Tuesday is ripped. Not that that has anything to do with anything since she's too surly to have a conversation with, and won't stop pissing Sutton off.

Sutton's life gets interesting after she dares Tuesday to make it through one yoga class, and then Tuesday gives Sutton the same dare. Soon enough they're spending time working out together and when the sweat starts flowing, the sparks start flying. How is it possible to be so attracted to a person you can barely stand?

But when someone from Tuesday's past shows up and Sutton sees a whole new side of Tuesday, will she change her mind about her grumpy landlord? Can she?

Chapter One

"Now, everyone relax into your savasana," I said, turning the lights all the way down. Soft sighs filled the room and I braced myself for the noise. There it was, like clockwork. Every day at precisely four fifty-five, the music would start from downstairs and would continue for several hours. Bass thumping, unbearably loud. Not the best way to end a yoga class.

I clenched my teeth and tried to ignore the vibrations coming up from below. This was unbearable. Pacing the room, I saw a few people wince at an especially loud thump. I wasn't going to be able 'om' my way out of this one.

With a final, "Namaste," that you could barely hear over the sounds from downstairs, I ended class. Outwardly, I kept a serene smile on my face. Inwardly, I was screaming. I hung around to talk to a few of my students, especially the new ones who were still unsure if they could handle a heated yoga class. I reassured and gave suggestions and tried to ignore the noise by making jokes about it. Once everyone was gone and I'd cleaned the studio, I went back to my office to work on a few things, but my concentration was shot for today.

Two months ago, I'd been informed that my building,

which I had been leasing for over a year and a half on the second floor, had been sold and the new owner was putting in a gym downstairs. Somehow, I'd made it through the construction, but that had just been the beginning.

Slamming my laptop shut, I decided to call it a day, for now. I didn't have to teach again tonight, but I should stay at the studio and make sure everything was functioning smoothly. I'd been running myself ragged for two years to get this business off the ground and I wasn't going to slow down anytime soon. I grabbed a coconut water from the fridge and angrily unscrewed the lid, dropping the whole thing on the floor in the process.

"Fuck," I said, grabbing a towel to mop it up. As a rule, I didn't curse in the studio, but I had been breaking more and more of my own rules lately. The bass from the speakers downstairs turned up, and I could feel it vibrating my bones and rattling my teeth.

"That's it," I said, throwing the coconut water in the trash. If I couldn't control the fact that my inner peace had been violated, at least I could ask them to turn the fucking music down.

I took one cleansing breath before I walked down the stairs and pushed through the glass door to the new gym. It was a punch in the gut to look at what had formerly been an adorable coffee shop and co-working space that had been completely ripped open and laid bare. Thick spongy tiles that alternated black and purple covered the floor, with the walls painted a harsh white and gray that reminded me of a prison. Ropes and rings hung from the ceiling and weight plates were everywhere. The whole thing smelled like lemon and rubber.

Only one person stood in the room. All that noise for just one person. They had their back to me with a weight bar resting on their upper back, giant black weight plates on either end. Slowly, they squatted down and then pressed back up to standing.

I forgot about the music for a second while I watched their legs flex. The person only wore shorts and a sports bra, and their back glistened with sweat in the low light. This place was definitely in need of some more lighting. The dim corners added more to the prison vibe.

The person squatted again, making a little grunting noise as they stood up again. I should probably stop staring, or at least make my presence known. I *definitely* needed to stop staring at the person's ass, even though it was a spectacular ass.

"Excuse me," I said, but they couldn't hear me over the music, so I stepped closer. "Excuse me!" I yelled, and the person slowly pivoted, weight bar still on their back. Dark hair, tan skin, piercing blue eyes. That was all I got, and I almost stumbled backwards. I'd never seen someone so intimidating in my life.

"You shouldn't sneak up behind people when they're lifting heavy things," she said, popping the bar off her back and letting it slam onto the floor and bounce a few times. She walked over to the sound system and turned the music down. Blessed relief. I could finally hear myself think.

"I'm sorry, I didn't know how else to get your attention. The music was a little loud."

One dark eyebrow raised.

"Can I help you?" The irritation radiated off her in waves. What if I was a potential customer? Not a very good first impression for this gym.

"Yes, I own the studio upstairs," I said, pointing upward, "and your music is too loud. It's messing with my classes." Her eyes narrowed.

"Is it," she said, and it wasn't a question.

"Yes. The bass pounds through the floor and it's distracting.

It was hard enough with the construction, but I thought once that was over, things would go back to normal." I'd never had issues with my downstairs neighbors before. They'd even given me free croissants every time I'd come in, and a few of their baristas had come to class. I wasn't getting any free croissants now. Just dirty looks and layers of hostility.

"Look, I'm not asking a lot. Just turn it down. Or get some headphones. Are you planning to make it that loud when you open?" I hoped not.

She stepped over the bar and walked closer to me, but it was only to reach for a water bottle that sat on a bench beside where I stood. I took an involuntary step back.

"I'm planning to do whatever I want," she said, taking a swig of water. "This is my gym." I blinked at her. I was not anticipating any kind of resistance. Why was she being like this? If the situation were reversed, I'd be so embarrassed and would have been apologizing over and over. I would have been completely ashamed of letting my music intrude into someone else's peace.

Not so much with her.

"Okayyyy," I said, drawing the word out. "So, what do you expect me to do?" She shrugged and took another swig of water.

"Find another building?" Now I was getting pissed. This was ridiculous. Just turn the damn music down and be done with it.

I inhaled angrily through my nose.

"Can you just be a nice person and turn the music down. Please? I'm asking you, as your upstairs neighbor, and as a human being on this planet. Please." I tried not to let too much begging enter my voice. I wasn't going to grovel. I might look like a sweet-as-pie yogi, but if you pushed my buttons, be prepared for me to burn everything down.

She sighed and rolled her eyes toward the ceiling. As if I was asking for too much.

"I'll do my best," she said, and I guessed that was as good as it was going to get. She turned her back on me and started doing pull-ups on one of the bars to my right.

"Nice talking to you," I said, before I turned on my heel and walked out. What an asshole. I hoped I never had to interact with her again.

"Wait," a voice said, just as I was about to yank the door open.

"What?" I said, snapping and swiveling around.

"Who are you?" The question was more of an accusation.

"I'm Sutton. I own Breathe Yoga, and *that*," I said, pointing to the sound system, "is really harshing my mellow."

Her eyes narrowed and her lips twitched.

"Harshing your mellow? Are you a time traveler from 1995?"

"No," I said. "And who are *you*?"

"I'm Tuesday, and I'm your new landlord."

Oh, shit.

"YOU BOUGHT THE BUILDING?" She looked about my age, or maybe a little older. Who the hell was in their mid-twenties and had building-buying money? In Boston, no less. I didn't need to be a real estate agent to know what the numbers might be on that.

"Yes, this is my building."

"And your name is Tuesday?" I couldn't have heard her right.

"Also true," she said, her eyes narrowing once again as she

glared at me. I wished I could take a step back, but my back was up against the door.

Her eyes dared me to make any comments about her name. I wouldn't dare. I wasn't that brave, and I valued my life too much. This girl could crush me without even breaking a sweat. Clearly, she used the gym as well as owning it. My eyes skipped along the acres of muscles on display and I knew I was staring too much, but I had to give her props; her body was impressive. From one fitness professional to another.

"Is there anything else?" she asked, after a tense silence. My gaze found its way back up to her eyes. They really were remarkable. And terrifying. This person could destroy my entire business if she wanted to. I had to tread lightly.

"No," I said, sounding breathless. "Nothing." I fumbled for the door handle and it took me a few seconds to realize that I had to pull instead of push. I thought I heard the sounds of a low laugh, but I probably imagined it as I scurried back upstairs and tried to remember how to breathe.

I DIDN'T GET HOME until late that night because I stayed to take the last yoga class. My body and my brain needed an hour and fifteen minutes of not thinking about my newest predicament, worrying about the future, or thinking about how I was going to move the business forward. Having five hundred tabs open in my mind at all times came in handy, but it was also completely exhausting.

My two kitties, Mocha and Cappuccino, meowed at me as if they hadn't seen me in five hundred years.

"Hello, babies," I said, picking up Mocha and nuzzling the little fluffball.

"They've been horribly abused," Zee, my roommate, said as they came out of the kitchen with a bag of chips.

"Hey, aren't those mine?" I asked, and they just shrugged.

"I'll replace them." I sighed and picked up Cappy. There was nothing like cuddling kittens after an awful day.

"You're home late," Zee said, flopping down on the couch. We'd been roommates since college and we were so comfortable with one another, living with Zee was the next best thing to living alone.

"Yeah, long day." I collapsed on the couch and motioned for them to hand me the bag of chips. I grabbed a handful and stuffed them in my face. I hadn't had dinner yet and I was starving. Zee had already eaten much earlier, and I didn't feel like heating up leftovers. I pulled out my phone and ordered a late-night pizza before looking at Zee again. Both kittens jumped into my lap and pawed at my shirt.

I thought about telling Zee about my encounter, but something made me say instead, "What about you? How was work?"

Zee worked at a queer youth center and did grant-writing work on the side.

"Good. Had this baby trans girl come in and she was so sweet. Didn't say a word, but she grabbed a book and sat and read the whole thing. She was the last one in the reading room when I was leaving. I tried to talk to her, but she ran away before I could get any information. I hope she'll come back." Zee told me some more stories from the day and my pizza arrived. They'd finished the bag of chips, and their eyes lit up when the doorbell rang and I said I'd gotten pizza.

"Pepperoni?" they asked.

"Yup," I said, as I walked up the stairs with the box.

"You're sharing, right?" they said.

"Don't I always?" I flipped open the box and they went right for a slice.

"Hold on, let me get some paper towels. And maybe a plate?"

"Plates are for losers," Zee said through a mouthful. I dashed to the kitchen and got two plates and paper towels. By the time I got back, Zee was already shoving a second piece of pizza in their mouth.

"You gonna leave some for me?" I asked as I shoved a plate at them. They took it begrudgingly.

"Yeah, I was only going to eat two pieces." Zee had never eaten just two pieces of pizza in their entire life. I would believe that when I saw it.

"You seem tense. What's up?" Zee asked. In addition to eating all of my food, Zee was also too perceptive for their own good.

"Met my landlord today," I said, staring at my first piece. Suddenly I wasn't as ravenous as I'd been five minutes ago.

"Oh, do tell," Zee said, going for another slice of pizza. Of course they could sense that there was something *to* tell.

"Well, I might have to find a new space for my studio. There was an encounter and I think I'm safe in saying that she's kind of an asshole. Also, what twenty-something has enough money to lease an entire fucking building in Boston?"

Zee pointed at me with their pizza slice.

"Someone with rich parents. That's probably it. You know, rich kids who have too much ennui because they've been handed everything ever. I guarantee it. Or, like, she won the lottery, but I doubt that. I bet she's from money." Ugh. Just what I needed.

"I'm sure it will be fine. Maybe she just had an off day? I'd just keep interactions to a minimum for a while. She might be a completely different person on another day. Maybe she was hangry. You know how I get when I need to eat." Yes, I did. If Zee didn't fuel themselves constantly, they got nasty. Normally they were the fluffiest sweetheart, but catch them when they were hungry? Run. Run away. Save yourself.

"I guess. I'm just worried she's going to want to kick me out." My brain liked to play out the worst possible scenario in excruciating detail. I could look forward to those thoughts at three in the morning when I couldn't sleep.

Why had I gone downstairs? Why couldn't I just have let her play her crappy loud music?

On the other hand, why did she have to be so hostile? I wasn't asking her to do anything outrageous.

Zee pressed their finger to the space right between my eyes.

"You need to stop that right now." Of course they knew I was spiraling and making this one interaction into something worthy of a movie plot and an award-winning script.

"I know, I know," I said, putting my plate down. Zee and I had demolished the medium pizza and now all I wanted was to go to bed and bask in my cheese coma with maybe a movie or a podcast and a book.

"Come here, my friend," Zee said, holding their arms out. I fell into them. Zee had long arms, so they gave the best hugs. I let myself fall into their embrace and closed my eyes. Their short brown hair tickled my cheek. Hugging Zee was the same feeling I had during savasana after an intense yoga class. Peace. Complete and total serenity.

"Let me know if you need me to slice her with my wit, because if she's a gym rat, I'm guessing she could probably kick my ass," Zee said into my hair. I laughed as I released them from the hug.

"I'll keep that in mind." I picked up the kitties and took them back to my bedroom. I needed to be covered in fluffballs right now. Ever since my cat, Mr. Fluffy, died at the ripe old age of eighteen, I'd been desperate for a new cat in my life. As a surprise one day, Zee asked me to meet them at the local shelter because they were overrun with kittens, and told me to pick one since they were sick of seeing me so sad. I came home with two kittens and was close to taking a third, but Zee put their foot down about that. I still had plans to sneak back and maybe smuggle a third kitten home when they were at work.

The kitties cried until I made a little nest of blankets on the bed for them and then they curled into little rolls and went right to sleep. I tried not to cry at how cute they were.

None of my podcasts were grabbing me, so I put on an Audrey Hepburn movie I'd seen a thousand times and scrolled through my phone for a new book. I'd finished one last night and it was the last in a series, so I wanted to start something new.

There was a brand-new release that I'd forgotten I preordered, and I made a little squealing noise when I saw that it was in my library. And then I checked to make sure I hadn't woken the babies. Nope, they were still twitching in their sleep.

Giddy, I started reading, but five minutes in, I realized I desperately needed some tea, so I gingerly removed myself from the bed without waking the kittens and tiptoed to the kitchen as quietly as I could. Zee was already in their room and I could see the glow of the television from under their door.

I grabbed some lemon ginger and popped it in my cup after I'd microwaved the water.

My mind had been drifting, thinking about my new book and how much I loved my kitties, and how I needed to cut my hair, or get some more blonde highlights in it. Nothing in particular. And then a pair of intense blue eyes blocked everything out. I forgot what I was doing for a moment.

Tea. Bed. Book.

I went back to my room and tried to shake the image.

Tuesday. Tuesday with the chiseled arms and hardcore eyes and hostility, who owned my building and could make my life a living hell and who had the greatest ass I'd ever seen on a person.

I was in so far over my head.

Chapter Two

THE GYM WAS dark when I walked by it on the way up to the studio the next morning. What a relief. Still, I saw a sign on the door that said OPENING SOON and that made me worry. The only person (probably) working out there now was Tuesday, so what was going to happen when there was a whole gym full of Tuesdays? I didn't even want to think about it.

Instead, I cleaned the studio and tried to meditate for a little while. It . . . did not happen. Sometimes brains were assholes and didn't want to do what we told them to. Especially when you had ADHD, like me. I tried for twenty minutes and then gave up, but it was fine because my first class was starting. I only had two instructors (other than me), so I ended up teaching most of the classes in a week, and on the weekends. It almost made me want to go back in time and slap some sense into myself when I'd thought, *sure, I can totally own and operate my own yoga studio in Boston. No big deal. I've got this!*

Both my parents were entrepreneurs, owning a restaurant and a computer repair shop. They'd worked so hard my entire life, and I wanted to be like them when I grew up. Turns out, all that hard work was actually hard.

I made it through most of the day without incident, but I kept my ear trained to the floor to feel if any music started up.

Nothing. I took a break to get some food and went past the gym, glancing in quickly. The lights were on, and people were walking around inside. Looked like they were painting or something. Good, the place definitely needed it. I understood the whole cinderblock chic thing was an aesthetic, but that wasn't the kind of gym that I would ever want to work out in.

When I came back almost an hour later, the door was open and the entryway reeked of paint fumes. I nearly choked on my way upstairs. It never ended. If it wasn't the music, it was *this*. I lit a ton of incense and breathed through my mouth. Class let out, and people wrinkled their noses as I made apologies for the smell.

By the end of the night I was a little high from the fumes and had the makings of an epic headache pounding in my skull. I headed home earlier than I normally would have and glanced over my shoulder at the gym on my way out. One of the previously gray walls was now a stark white, which was an improvement, I guess? Maybe there would be a mural or logo or something. The place was going to be called CrossFit 721, according to the posters. Not the most auspicious name, but I couldn't really talk. I strayed away from any bad yoga puns when I'd been naming my place and I'd picked the most generic thing I could think of.

"Enjoying the view?" a voice said behind me, and I swear my soul left my body for a second.

"What the fuck?" I gasped and turned around to find Tuesday watching me. Once I got my breathing under control again, I noticed that she was covered in flecks of white paint.

"That's not a very zen thing to say, is it?" she said, raising one paint-spattered brow. Her hair was up in a bun, but the paint had made its way there as well, like little bits of snow.

"It is when someone sneaks up behind me," I said, with my hand on my pounding heart. "Were you painting?"

"Is it that obvious?" she said, her voice dry. I couldn't get a read on her. Was she just an asshole, or was there something else to this girl named Tuesday?

"Sorry, I was just on my way out. Checking things out," I said. I had never wished for teleportation to be a thing more than at this moment so I could be back in my apartment in the blink of an eye.

Tuesday rolled her shoulders and for the first time I noticed there were dark circles etched under her eyes. I had a flashback of when I was first opening the studio and I'd been covered in paint as well. I hadn't been able to afford a crew to paint, so I'd done it all myself, with the help of Zee and a few other friends on weekends. It had been awful and fun at the same time, as most things were.

Tuesday tilted her head to the side and regarded me in a way that made my cheeks get hot.

"What?" I finally said, when she wasn't forthcoming.

"Do you want to help?"

I blinked at her, unsure if I'd heard her right.

"Excuse me?"

"Do you want to help? I've got brushes. And I can order dinner."

"You can't be serious," I blurted out. Yesterday she'd been nothing but rude and now . . . I didn't even know what to do with this.

"Suit yourself," she said, pushing past me. "I'm going to be cranking the music, so things might get loud anyway." The door shut in my face before I could say anything.

What the fuck was her problem?

"SO, she was asking for labor in exchange for dinner?" Zee asked later, their brown eyes wide as we sat on the couch dissecting the encounter. I couldn't *not* tell Zee about this one. It was just so strange. I'd turned the situation over and over in my mind on my drive home, but I wasn't any closer to understanding what that had all been about.

"I mean, I guess? It seemed like the weirdest peace offering I've ever heard of, but maybe she was just trying to be an asshole again. I have no idea. I can't get a read on her and it's really starting to irritate me. I've only had two encounters with this person, and they've both left me annoyed and puzzled." I made a frustrated noise and was about to ask Zee what they thought again, but found them watching me.

"What?" I asked. I didn't like that look they were giving me. Slowly, they smiled. "What is it? You're freaking me out, Zee."

"You're attracted to her." I made a sputtering noise like a car trying to start in the winter before I was able to formulate any words.

"I am not!" I said, and my voice squeaked on the last word.

Zee cackled and scared the kittens, who rolled around on the floor with some new toys that we bought them.

"You totally are. I mean, I read between the lines and figured out she was hot, but your little obsession with her is telling me that she's *really* hot." I pressed my lips together because I didn't want to say anything that might incriminate myself and lead Zee to think their theory was something that it wasn't.

Okay, fine. Tuesday was stunning. Gorgeous. Hot. Sexy. All of those. But that didn't mean anything. I saw hot people all the time; I ran a yoga studio. Her attractiveness had nothing to do with anything.

"Ohhhh, this is very interesting," Zee said, stroking their chin and staring at me as I glared back.

"Stop it," I said, pointing my finger in their face. "Stop it right now." They laughed and shook their head.

"No way. She's mean and hot, which is a deadly combination. You'd better be careful. Pretty soon she's going to ask you to 'help paint' and there will be no brushes or paint involved. Unless she's into that kind of thing." I stood up from the couch.

"I'm leaving right now unless you stop talking about this immediately. And I'm taking the babies with me." I scooped up both kittens and held them to my chest as they wiggled, angry I'd taken them away from their new shiny toys.

"No, don't leave," Zee said, falling horizontal on the couch and reaching for me dramatically. "Come backkkkkk."

I turned on my heel and pretended to flounce, whipping my hair around.

"Come back and I'll let you have the rest of the ice cream," they said. That did it. I went back and dropped the kittens in their lap. They made cooing noises at them and gave them kisses as they meowed.

"I'm not attracted to her," I said. "I just need you to know that. I'm not."

"Uh huh," Zee said, not looking at me, but pretending to be consumed by the kittens, "I *completely* believe you."

I wanted to throw something at them, but I also didn't want to hit the babies, so I just huffed off to the kitchen to get the ice cream and then returned.

"What are we watching?" Zee turned on the TV and flipped through our different streaming services.

"This one again?" she asked, landing on our favorite show that we'd watched at least four or five times through already.

"Yup," I said, digging my spoon into the ice cream

container. The show was a classic that had been out when we were younger and hadn't exactly aged well, but we still adored it.

I found Zee eyeing me a few times and I could tell that they wanted some of the ice cream.

"You said I could have it," I said, not looking at them.

"I know, I'm having regrets now." I sighed and handed it over. "One bite."

"Thank youuuuu. Did you know that you're the best? Because you are. The best." They took the biggest bite ever and then handed the container back.

"I know I am," I said. Mocha and Cappy toddled over to me and pawed at the ice cream container.

"This isn't for kitties," I said, holding it so they could sniff the contents. Of course, they both recoiled and meowed at me in confusion. "I know, life is confusing, my babies." I finished the ice cream and set the container down where they couldn't get at it. I petted a kitten with each hand, which made them both purr.

I wasn't attracted to Tuesday. Not with her attitude. Hot and mean. That was a way to describe her. I could admit she was hot without that indicating I was attracted to her. Right? That was a thing.

Mocha bumped my hand with her head and I realized I'd been slacking on my petting duties.

"I'm sorry, I'm sorry," I said, and scratched her head right where she liked it. "I'm a bad kitty mom." Mocha yawned in response.

I DIDN'T KNOW what I was going to walk in to the next day, but I braced myself for anything. Tuesday wasn't there in the morning, as expected, but the painters were back again when I went to get some lunch. This time I scanned the room and saw her dark bun. She was right alongside the painters with a roller in her hand and paint smeared all over her thighs. I'd never seen thighs quite like hers. They popped out so much I wondered if she needed to let out her pants to accommodate them.

There were enough painters so it seemed like she could leave them to it, but I bet she didn't trust them to get things right and wanted to be there to supervise. That had been how I was with my studio. Even if I'd had the money to hire more people, I would have been hovering over every little thing and making sure it turned out right.

Maybe Tuesday and I had more in common than I thought.

I spared a moment for that thought, but then she turned around and her blue eyes shot right toward me. Crap, I'd been caught staring at her again, and creeping on her business. I didn't mean to. It just kind of happened.

Tuesday's eyes narrowed imperceptibly, but she didn't do anything else. I hurried away and didn't look toward the door when I came back. Just kept my eyes on the stairs.

I was finishing checking people in for one of the other teachers when someone came up the stairs and I did a double take.

"What are you doing here?" I asked. The class had started so I didn't have to think about any of the yogis seeing whatever this was going to be.

"Just checking things out," she said, looking around as if she'd been thrown into a room on another planet. I wondered if that was the same look on my face when I walked into her gym.

"Do you want a tour?" I asked, hoping she would say no.

"Sure," she said, concentrating on me again. Her eyes really were remarkable. The clear blue of a frozen lake.

"Can you take your shoes off?" I asked, and she hesitated for a second, but then slipped off her paint-covered running shoes. She wasn't wearing any socks.

I stepped out from behind the desk and approached her. I gave tours of the studio all the time to new clients, but this was different. I hoped she wouldn't see the slightly stained ceiling tiles that I kept putting off replacing, or the scuffs on the walls that I needed to clean and repaint, or the way the floor was just a little warped. Granted, she was my landlord and it was her duty to fix that shit. What a weird situation.

"So, uh, this is where people check in," I said, gesturing to the desk that I'd been sitting behind. "And we have retail." Worst tour ever. I couldn't look at Tuesday while I gave her the pathetic tour, including the snack and drink area with kombucha and green juice taps and a hot water dispenser for assorted teas.

"Class is in session in this studio, but I can show you the other one." I'd lucked out in that this place had already been fitted to be a yoga studio, complete with two heated rooms that could also be used for workshops, etc. I opened the door and showed Tuesday the smaller, unoccupied room.

"Nice," she said, but I couldn't tell if she was saying that, or if she really meant it.

We finished the tour and went back to the reception area.

"That's pretty much it," I said, glancing up at the logo on the wall. I'd ordered a decal from a shady company online and had put it up myself. It was still a bit wrinkled in places. Yet another thing to fix.

"Nice, nice," Tuesday said. "You've really done a good job. If I did yoga at all, this is the kind of place I would want to come."

"Thank you," I said. That meant a lot. "How is your place coming along?" It only seemed polite to ask.

Her shoulders slumped, just a millimeter.

"It's coming. Slowly."

"Do you think you're going to be ready to open?" I probably shouldn't ask that, but it was a relief to be having a somewhat normal conversation with her.

"We will be," she said, and her eyes snapped back on me. The moment of weakness I'd seen a few seconds ago was gone. Her shoulders tensed again. Tuesday was back in charge.

"We?" I asked. So far, I'd only seen her and the painting crew.

"I should go," she said, edging toward the stairs.

"Okay," I said. "See you later?" This interaction added even more confusion to the picture I was trying to paint of Tuesday. I didn't even know her last name.

"Maybe," she said, pivoting and jogging down the stairs.

I shook my head to clear it. Every single time I had an encounter with Tuesday, it was like I was thrown into an alternate universe where I didn't know any of the rules, what to say, or how to act. She completely confused me in so many ways. It didn't help that her body was so appealing. That was distracting enough. Muscles on top of muscles on top of muscles. It was just excessive and unnecessary and . . .

Arousing. I could admit that to myself now. I wouldn't admit it to anyone else, not even Zee, but yeah. Hot as fuck was Tuesday. Hot and mean, Zee had said, and Tuesday had both of those in excess.

Although, the mean had been dulled a little bit today. I couldn't work out why she'd come up here, what her purpose had been. Was she trying to be nice after the music thing?

I didn't know. I sat at the desk and was working on figuring it out as I answered customer emails when I heard it.

The steady throb of a bass beat hit the bottoms of my bare feet and I thought I was hallucinating for a moment. Nope. There it was. The music was back. So much for Tuesday being nice. I waited a few minutes for the music to stop, but it did not. No, it got a little bit louder.

I wanted to scream. What an asshole. I only hesitated for two minutes before I was back down the stairs and pushing open the door of the gym.

The paint fumes weren't as strong, but there was still one wall that needed to be done. All the rest were stark white. Now the place looked like some kind of hospital basement.

"Seriously?" I yelled over the music. She turned around slowly from the wall she'd been working on with a roller.

"Oh, can I help you?" she said. As if I'd come down here to ask her if she wanted a cup of tea.

"Yeah, you can turn down the music. Again. What is wrong with you?" I shook a little with my anger. I didn't usually have such a hot button, but Tuesday seemed to know exactly what to do to get me mad. It wasn't just what she was *doing*, it was her attitude about it. Like I'd intruded on *her* and was the one in the wrong.

"Wouldn't you like to know," she said, putting down the roller. "I'll be done in a little while." I was about to ask her why she couldn't turn the music down right-the-fuck now when she stripped off her white tank and was left only in a black sports bra and I forgot how to make words.

I could do laundry on those abs. There was no way they were real. They had to be painted on or tattooed. I felt myself gaping.

"You could make it go faster by helping," she said, tossing the tank to the side.

"No," I said, finally formulating a word. "Do you not care

that you're annoying my clients and potentially hurting my business?"

She rolled her eyes a little and then walked over to the sound system, turning it down a few notches.

"Better?"

"I guess," I said. I needed to get back upstairs because class would be getting out, but I found myself with my feet glued to the floor. Why couldn't I move?

"Anything else?" she asked, when I didn't immediately leave.

"Yes," I said, because I needed a plausible reason to still be down here.

"And?" she replied, when I wasn't forthcoming.

"You should come to yoga." It was the first thing I could think of to say. "We offer the first class for free." Now I definitely needed to run away.

Tuesday seemed surprised by my declaration.

"Really?" she asked as if she didn't believe me. "You want me to come do yoga?" Without even trying, my brain conjured an image of Tuesday in downward dog with me adjusting her hips and I had to close my eyes and breathe for a second. Mean. She was mean. Hot, but mean. The mean had to outweigh the hot.

"Yes. Yoga is an amazing workout for the mind and the body." I wasn't going to pull up the studies about the benefits of yoga right now, but if she asked me, I would. I had the receipts.

"I'm sure it is, but I like doing a *real* workout. Stretching is good, but it's not going to build a body like lifting does." Oh, now I was *mad*.

"You wouldn't last an entire advanced class. Not a chance." I offered one advanced class a week, as well as a few intermediate, but everything else was basic for all levels of people. Actually, she might not even make it through the basic class. I'd seen her type before: cocky gym rats that thought yoga was just a bunch of fancy poses that did nothing, before they took their first class. After, they would come to me, drenched in sweat with shaky knees and telling me that I was completely right and they didn't know how intense the workout was going to be. Tuesday wouldn't be any different, and I wanted to be there to see when it happened.

"Is that a dare? I never turn down a dare. Ever." I always ran away from dares, as a rule. Seriously, I would pretend at sleepovers that my mom needed me home if girls wanted to play Truth or Dare. Because you couldn't pick truth or else you'd get teased relentlessly. It was easier to just go home. But right now, a dare was tasting pretty good. Like cake in bed after being fucked really well. Mmmm. Great, now I was thinking about fucking. I did not need to be thinking about fucking around Tuesday.

"Yes," I finally said. "It is a dare. Our class schedule is online. See you in an intermediate class," I said, finally unsticking my feet from the floor that was covered in sheets of plastic to save it from getting covered in paint. Not that the floor was anything to write home about anyway. A little bit of paint might improve it.

"I'll be there," she said, and I glanced over my shoulder. I wanted to leave her with one last zinger.

"Oh, did I mention I'm the teacher? You can rent a mat if you don't have one." I knew she didn't have a yoga mat. I shut the door and walked up the stairs on a cloud of triumph.

She was going to crash and burn and it would be perfect payback. I couldn't wait.

Chapter Three

I was on a high from that encounter for the next two days. It was the weekend, but I didn't see any evidence of her. I tried to take some time off from work, so I went to a movie with Zee, and then took myself out for a fancy dinner, which I liked to do at least once a month. Sitting alone at a restaurant didn't bother me. I loved having a glass of wine and a nice meal and not having to talk to anyone. Sometimes I even brought a book. Sure, I got strange looks and the waiter or waitress always asked if I was alone or waiting for someone, but whatever. I deserved to get dressed up and have pasta with truffles and tiramisu. No one else was going to take me out.

I hadn't had a girlfriend in ages, and never one that was really serious. I was just so busy with work that most of the time I didn't mind. It was only every now and then when I saw other couples holding hands, or when I was in bed alone (with the exception of the kittens) that I wanted someone there. And definitely after a long day at the studio when I was crunching the numbers and wondering how I was going to pay my expenses that month. Thankfully, I had Zee for a lot of that stuff, but it would be different with a girlfriend. Zee was between boyfriends right now, so we were both living the single life.

When I came home after taking myself out for the most incredible sashimi and hand rolls followed by green tea mochi in the city, Zee was on the floor with the kittens.

"How was your date?" they said, looking up. I slipped off my heels and got down on the floor. I made it a rule that I had to wear my prettiest clothes when taking myself out, and that included heels.

"Excellent. I'm so full." I put my hand on my belly and lay back on the floor. The kitties meowed and climbed all over my purple velvet jumpsuit.

"I want to go on a date," they said, laying down next to me.

"Find a guy, go on date. I think that's how it works?" I'd never been super successful at dating. Nearly all of my girlfriends had approached me and made the first move. I always ended up tongue-tied and too nervous in the presence of a pretty lady.

"I'm so picky about guys, you know this. I wish we knew more people." It was true; we did tend to stay in our apartment a lot.

"I can see if there's anyone at the studio. Dude yogis tend to be pretty chill." Sometimes a little *too* chill, in my opinion.

"No, that's fine. I can find my own boyfriends, thanks. What about you and girlfriends? Anyone new? Other than the hot and mean one?" I sat up.

"Are you talking about Tuesday? Because she is not girlfriend material. I don't even know if she's queer, anyway." I had my suspicions, but I didn't know for sure. I had learned from experience not to assume until someone told you flat out who they were.

"I bet she is. I have a feeling." I didn't let them see me roll my eyes. They were always having "feelings" about things and, a lot of the time, they were wrong.

"Remember your feelings about Jessica?" I asked, shuddering. I'd gone on exactly three dates with her and it had been a complete disaster. Turned out Jessica was married and thought that it was just fine for her to be stepping out on her husband with me because they'd had a threesome once and he watched lesbian porn. I wasn't sure if I would ever recover from that date.

"Okay, so I was wrong about that. Really wrong." She plucked Mocha from my stomach and kissed her little head.

"So, so wrong," I said.

"But I'm not wrong about this," Zee said. I groaned.

"Can we stop talking about this now?" I hadn't told Zee about the bet I'd made with Tuesday. Our next intermediate class was, ironically, on Tuesday night. Two days away. I had no idea if she would show up or not, mostly because I didn't have a read on anything she would do. The dare seemed like something . . . private? I didn't know. Maybe I just didn't want to hear comments or dissect the whole thing with Zee. I'd tell them after it happened. If it did.

"Sure, my love," they said. "Wanna see my new project?" They sat up and scrambled to their little craft corner in the living room. Zee did all kinds of amazing art, but lately they'd gotten into embroidery. It sounded like something a grandmother would do, but I doubted a ton of grandmothers would embroider the word "fuck" surrounded by pretty flowers.

"You like?" they said, bringing over their embroidery hoop. "It's a commission." It was halfway done, with the rest of the words outlined and the flowers around the quote started. It said, "This place is a shithole." I burst out laughing as I read it.

"Nice. Very nice."

"I'm also doing a "Stay Sexy, Don't Get Murdered" one for someone next week." I handed the hoop back to them.

"I need a hobby, but I'm bad at everything but watching too much Netflix," I said, groaning. Yoga had once been my hobby, but now it was my job and those weren't the same things. Sure, I still loved doing it, but it wasn't an activity I could just dip in and out of anymore. I had to LIVE yoga now.

"What about baking? Or cooking?" I glared at them.

"You just want me to make more food that you can eat."

They grinned at me and shrugged.

"I would never do that." I snorted.

"You would definitely do that."

"Maybe a little bit. Also, you're a shit cook, so I don't have much faith in your baking abilities." I smacked them in the shoulder, but it was true.

I wanted to find a hobby that would let me unwind from my job. I ran through all the things I'd tried and failed at before. They were numerous, and I had evidence of them sitting in our spare room to prove it.

"You'll figure it out," they said, patting my arm.

"Maybe I could be a kitten cuddler. That's a thing, I'm sure."

"Yeah, you could volunteer at the shelter. But you might have to pick up a lot of cat poop." We both made faces. Our kittens were so small still, but they pooped SO MUCH. It didn't seem possible that so much crap could come from such tiny beings.

"I don't know. I'll figure it out." I hung out on the floor for a little bit longer and then got up to shower and then covered my face in a sheet mask as I put on a documentary. I had the social life of a grandmother. All I needed to do was add knitting, which I had tried, and failed, already.

The kitties cried outside my door to come in. Zee didn't like sleeping with them because they tended to thrash in their sleep and was worried about squishing them, so the babies slept in my bed.

I scooped them up and they went right to sleep. I peeled off my sheet mask and tossed it.

Bored, I picked up my phone and scrolled through it, checking my personal accounts as well as the ones for the studio to make sure there wasn't anything bad in the comments of my posts. Once that was done, I found my fingers typing in the name for Tuesday's gym. She had a page that was sparse on information but had a logo. She was an admin on the page, so I found her last name for the first time.

Tuesday Grímsdóttir. Wow. If that wasn't a badass name, then I didn't know what was. Her last name was odd, so I looked up the origins. Icelandic. Interesting. With her dark hair and tan skin, she certainly didn't look Nordic at all. I skipped back to her personal page and couldn't see much. I would have to follow or friend her to see more. Damn. I definitely wasn't going to do that. Instead, I scrolled through what she had and then googled her, as you do. She'd competed in various CrossFit events, so she was there for that, and there were a few articles she'd written for various publications about training and nutrition. I skimmed a few of them and realized it was really fucking late and I had to teach first thing in the morning.

What did I do? I certainly didn't spend another hour looking her up online. Oh, wait, I did.

The next morning when my alarm rang, I groaned. I had two kittens on my chest, and they weren't happy about me waking up either.

"Noooo," I moaned. I'd spent too long stalking Tuesday online. What a childish thing to do. I wasn't a horny teenager looking up a crush. I was a grown woman. A business owner. I couldn't waste my time on such foolishness, and yet, I had.

"Your mommy needs some help," I said, kissing Cappy on her perfect little head. She just meowed in my face and then licked my nose.

"Very helpful, thank you," I said. Removing the kittens, I rolled my way out of bed and struggled to the bathroom. Zee was already in the kitchen and I fumbled my way to the cup of coffee they'd already made for me.

"Good morning, sunshine," they said, and I grunted. I wished I didn't have to teach classes in the morning. I wished I didn't have to hold classes this early, but just because I wasn't a morning person didn't mean other people weren't. I had a steady crew of early bird yogis who liked to come before work and start their day in the right mindset.

I sucked down my coffee like it was oxygen and then rested my head on Zee's shoulder as they made breakfast. They'd been cooking for both of us since I could remember, and I wasn't going to tell them to stop anytime soon.

"What are we having?" I said, waiting for the coffee to kick in. The kittens came out and cried for their food, even though their bowls were full. I calmly explained that to them and pointed to the bowls, but they would only quiet when I pretended to get them more food and mimed pouring it into the bowls.

"Egg, cheese, and spinach sandwiches on English muffins and some potatoes with avocado on top." They had said so many of my favorite words right there.

"Do you need me to do anything?" I said, but they just gave me a look.

"You could throw some chia seeds and collagen powder in my protein shake if you're really feeling frisky," they said. I laughed and grabbed their premade shake and added the items, shaking it up and handing it to them. We tried our best when it came to nutrition, but that didn't always work out, so we did our best when we could.

Zee served me, making the plate all fancy and shit and we headed to the living room to eat. There was space for a dining room in our apartment, but Zee was using it as their craft corner, and we didn't see the need for a dining table. Whenever we had people over, we always sat on the couch or the floor anyway.

By the time I was finished with breakfast, I had to get my ass moving. I threw on my yoga clothes, kissed the kitties goodbye, and gave Zee a wave as I headed to my car.

As soon as I got inside the studio, I started feeling better. There was just something about this space that made me happy. Maybe because it was the culmination of so many dreams I'd had of owning my own business.

I'd always known that I would, but I didn't know what kind of business that would be. It wasn't until college that I went to my first yoga class and I thought I might be good at it. I'd saved my money and had done several seminars taught by amazing yoga experts and really knew that was what I wanted to do. And here I was, years later, with my own studio.

I lit the incense and made sure the yoga blocks were lined up and everything was ready for the first class. My students started coming in and I greeted most of them by name. There were two newbies and I gave them a tour, albeit a much better one than I'd given Tuesday.

Once I was in teacher mode, I wasn't thinking about anything but calling the poses, assisting where needed, and making sure the heat was up and everyone was blissing out by the time we got to savasana. It was freedom and peace for a little while.

And then class was over and I had to go out to the reception area and was reminded of Tuesday. I wondered if she was downstairs right now. I wondered what time she'd gotten up today and if she was still painting. I wondered what her middle name was, if she had one, and if she liked or hated pineapple on pizza, and if she was single or into girls. Perfectly regular things to wonder about a person you'd spent several hours looking up online into the wee hours of the morning.

Ellen, who taught the next class and had been one of my first yoga friends, came out of the elevator.

"Wow," I said, taking in her hair.

"What do you think?" She said, using her walker to do a little twirl. Her hair, which had been dyed a shade of blue last time I saw her, was now a bright orange that totally worked for her. It wouldn't look good on many people, but Ellen pulled it off.

"You look adorable," I said. She beamed and came over to the benches to take her shoes off.

"Need any help?" I asked. She had a progressive spinal condition and some days she used her walker or a cane and some days she didn't.

"Nope, I got it," she said, sliding off her sneakers. "How many do we have signed up?" I checked the computer.

"Ten as of right now, so hopefully we'll get a few more." Our classes during the day were quieter than the evening classes, but sometimes more would show up on holidays, or when the colleges weren't in session.

"Sounds good," she said, and then put her hair up. "Wait a second."

"What?" I said, touching my face.

"Something is different." She squinted her eyes at me. I didn't know what she was talking about.

"Is there something wrong with my hair?" I used my hands to check it and then looked at my shirt.

"No, it's something else. Something in your energy." Ellen waved her hand in my general direction.

"What about my energy?" Ellen couldn't read my mind, but sometimes it felt like she could. I was cursed with being surrounded by people who were too perceptive for their own good. I couldn't hide *anything* from anyone.

"Not sure. But something is different. You're more fiery today."

"Are you sure it's not just your hair?" I asked with a smirk.

"Nope," she said, blowing a flyaway out of her face. "Something is different." We were interrupted by a few students coming up the stairs, so I went to set the heat for Ellen's class and get out the chairs that some of the students used. All our classes were accessible, but Ellen taught a few that were specifically for disabled people. She also taught workshops for disabled people and caregivers on the benefits of yoga.

In the rush to check everyone in and make sure the room was ready and the music was working, I didn't have time to think about what Ellen had said about my energy, but I did have time to think about how hungry I was. Working so much had really gotten me on a bad eating schedule, and some days I had to set timers to remind me to eat when I got consumed with tasks.

Deciding to go out and get a salad and fresh mango juice at the organic restaurant down the street, I jogged down the stairs and did a quick look over my shoulder at the gym. The door was open and the paint fumes were definitely lessened. From what I could see, all the walls were painted, and there was Tuesday, putting up a decal on the wall just like I had upstairs. I should just walk by and not say anything, but then I heard her make a sound of frustration. The decal was defeating her, and I couldn't just walk by and not help. Even if she was hot and mean.

"It's easier with two people," I said, and she whirled around so fast, she almost slammed her back into the wall.

"What the fuck?" I almost laughed at the shocked expression on her face.

"That's not a very nice thing for a gym owner to say, is it?" I said, crossing my arms. Her blue eyes narrowed and her lips twitched.

"Touché."

"Do you need some help? I've got experience with these." The decal she had was massive; it was at least eight feet wide by five feet tall. Impossible to put up on your own.

Tuesday pressed her lips together and considered me. She'd asked me for help before, but somehow I was guessing that having someone offer was different.

"Okay," she said, and I breathed a little sigh of relief. I didn't know how this was going to go, and I hoped she would tone down the mean a little bit. The music was on today, but at a lower volume.

"Music at an acceptable level, this is nice," I said. She sighed heavily.

"Is it going to be like this?" she asked. No. It didn't have to be. I gritted my teeth and gave her a tight smile. "Is that supposed to reassure me?"

"Look, if you don't want my help, I can just leave," I said, turning around. A warm hand held my arm. Her fingers flexed and I bet they could crush my bones. Everything about her was strong.

"No, no. I do need your help." I had been hoping for some kind of apology, but I guessed that was as good as it was going to get.

"Okay then," I said. "Have you sketched out where you want it to go?" She shook her head.

"I thought I would just put it up." I looked around and found a pencil on the ground.

"First we need to measure." Tuesday found a tape measure and we measured the logo, and then drew an outline on the wall with the pencil and I hopped on a ladder to line up the top and tape it.

"Now we just peel this back and hope for the best," I said. "We have to do this at the same time for it to work." I counted and we pulled the backing off the logo, pressing it to make sure it stuck on the wall, pushing out any bubbles that formed.

It took a while, and we barely spoke the whole time. My stomach growled and I was going to have to rush to have time to eat anything before my next class.

At last the logo was finished. Bold and purple and black, which I guess were the official colors of the gym. Not my taste, but it worked.

"Looks good," I said, and Tuesday squinted up at it.

"You think?"

"Yeah. It's very . . . aggressive." She turned and raised her eyebrows.

"What is that supposed to mean?" I got down off the ladder.

"Just what I said. That's the whole CrossFit thing, right? Aggressive military-style stuff? Sit-ups until you throw up blood?" I didn't know much about CrossFit, but that was the gist I'd gotten from anything I'd seen.

"Some of it can be like that, but this gym is going to be different," she said, folding up the ladder with a snap and leaning it against the wall.

"Different how?" I thought she was a franchise so would be beholden to the main entity. It was one of the main reasons I had decided not to franchise and go it on my own instead.

Tuesday didn't answer. Instead, she sat down on one of the wooden boxes that were stacked against the opposite wall.

"You want my business plan?" she asked. I looked toward the door.

"Are you always like this?" I asked. She blew out a breath.

"Yes," she said.

"You must be a delight at parties." I should leave. I was hungry and she wasn't being the nicest. Yet here I was again, with my feet stuck to the checkered floor.

"Not a big fan of parties. Prefer to stay home with my turtles." I blinked a few times.

"Turtles?" Had I heard her right?

"Never mind," she said, fiddling with the edge of the box and not looking at me.

I couldn't believe the next words that came out of my mouth. "Look, I'm going to get some lunch, do you want to come?"

What the hell?

Tuesday's head snapped up and she eyed me, suspicious.

"You want to take me out to lunch?"

"Yes?" It sounded like I wasn't sure at all, which was the truth.

"Okay," she said, slapping her ample thighs and standing up. "Where to?"

And that was how I found myself sitting across from Tuesday, my grumpy landlord, at my favorite lunch place.

"I haven't really gone around the neighborhood yet to find out what's here. This is nice." She picked up the menu and I didn't know what to say or do so I just kept pretending to read my own menu even though I'd been here so many times I already knew what I wanted.

The waiter came over and I knew he recognized me because I got takeout here almost every day.

"Hey, how's it going Sutton?" he asked, and I felt myself blushing and mumbling that things were going well. He'd even come to a few yoga classes in the past.

"What can I get for you?" he asked, and I ordered my usual of the house salad with goat cheese, a fresh pressed mango, orange, and peach juice, and a side of fries because I needed potatoes right now.

Tuesday got the steak strip salad, a side of sweet potato fries, a side of hummus and chips, a green juice, and a peanut butter chocolate protein shake. I tried not to stare, because the plates here weren't tiny. I almost never finished my salads when I got them. I was hoping to have the fries later on between evening sessions.

Tuesday stared right at me after she placed her order, as if daring me to say something. I had the feeling she wanted me to make a comment, so I didn't. I just handed the waiter my menu and pressed my lips together into a smile.

"Their salads are so good here. They don't skimp on anything," I said. Tuesday just grunted.

"So . . ." I said, my voice trailing off. I didn't know how to talk to someone like Tuesday. Where did I even start? "How is the gym going?" That seemed like the only topic I could think of to ask about.

"You don't have to do that," she said, and the waiter brought us water. I grabbed my glass and started drinking, if only for something to do.

"Do what?" I asked, after I'd nearly drained the whole glass.

"Do the small talk thing. It's insulting to both of us." I set my water down.

"I'm just trying to be nice," I said. "But I can sit here in silence if that's what you want. I don't even know why you came." I didn't want to sit in silence, but at least it gave me time to just stare at her body and wonder how she'd gotten it like that and how many hours a day she worked out and how much she could lift.

"I was hungry," she said. "I don't turn down food. Ever." To build those muscles, I was guessing she had to eat a lot.

"Fine," I said, wishing I had sipped my water more slowly. Instead I swirled the ice around in the glass, waiting for it to melt.

"I'm not good at people," she said. "It wasn't supposed to be like this." I looked up from my water and she was staring out the window.

"What do you mean?" She glanced back at me.

"Nothing."

"No, tell me," I said, surprised at my own boldness.

"It's fine," she said, waving me off. I made a huffing noise and she sighed.

"I wasn't supposed to be the one running the gym. I had a . . . business partner, and now I don't. There." Something about the way she said "business partner" told me there was much more to that story.

"What happened?" I asked.

"I don't want to talk about it," she said, picking up her napkin and starting to shred it. Guess we'd touched a nerve.

"That sucks, I'm sorry," I said, and I meant it. I'd thought about having a partner, but I was too worried that someone would screw me over. I generally believed the best in people, except where money was concerned. Then you never knew who you were really dealing with.

Our drinks came and Tuesday stayed lost in her thoughts and I had plenty of my own.

"Um, how long have you done yoga?" she asked after a little while. She sounded awkward asking the question, as if it was something she wasn't used to doing.

"Let me think, about five or six years now? I decided to take a class in college when I was completely stressed out and working three jobs. I thought it would be something I'd do once a week, but I kept coming back and coming back and I couldn't get enough. I decided that's what I wanted to dedicate my life to. Helping other people the way yoga helped me." I didn't care if that sounded sappy; it was the truth and I wasn't going to shy away from it. In fact, I hadn't told her the entire truth: yoga had saved my life.

"That's beautiful," she said, and I almost slid off my chair. I wasn't expecting that reaction.

"Thank you," I said, shocked. "When did you find Cross-Fit?" Her face fell and her mouth curved into a frown.

"Let's just say there was an ex involved," she finally said, as our food arrived. Hers took up three quarters of the table and I had to almost stack my plates on top of each other.

"Sorry," she mumbled, but I shook my head.

"It's fine."

"If it's any consolation, I'm going to be done with most of these in about five minutes," she said, stabbing her fork into a huge piece of steak on top of her salad.

"Good to know," I said, going for my fries first. I added extra salt and slathered them in ketchup. I didn't miss Tuesday making a face at the ketchup—that I ignored.

What followed was an eating performance that was both impressive and beautiful. I'd never been fascinated by someone eating before, but Tuesday was something else. The salad disappeared within moments, and then she systematically demolished every other plate in a methodical fashion. She had impeccable manners, didn't spill anything, and kept her napkin in her lap the whole time. Then there was me, who dropped a bunch of fries in my lap, got dressing on my shirt, and nearly knocked over my water glass three times. Tuesday eating was like ballet. Me eating was like a toddler who had just been handed a fork for the first time.

She finished everything and I still had a pile of fries left, and she was definitely eyeing them.

"Do you want some?" I asked, pushing the plate toward her. The waiter had cleared her finished plates ages ago.

"I would, but they're tainted now," she said.

"Don't like ketchup?" I asked, picking up a fry and dipping the entire thing in the pile of ketchup I'd added to the plate. I almost wanted more ketchup than fry sometimes. I had jumbo bottles of ketchup in my fridge right now because I was scared of running out. That would be the worst thing to ever happen to me.

"You might as well have put blood on those fries. Actually, blood would be preferable to the monstrosity known as ketchup." I narrowed my eyes and pointed at her with my ketchup-soaked fry.

"That is your opinion and I will not accept such negativity. Not in front of my precious fries." I put the fry in my mouth and then pretended to shield the rest of them with my body.

Tuesday blinked a few times at me and then her lips twitched, as if she was fighting a smile. Why couldn't she just let herself smile if she wanted to? It was so easy, why fight it? I still didn't understand her at all.

"It's not an opinion; it's a fact." I rolled my eyes.

"That's your opinion." We were going to get nowhere with this, but I was beginning to think she was doing this just to wind me up.

Tuesday shook her head and finished her smoothie.

"Are you full now?" I asked. She had to be. There was no way she could still be hungry.

"For a little while," she said, patting her stomach.

"How much do you have to eat in a day?" I couldn't imagine the grocery bills.

"Let's just say a lot," she replied. "It's more about the right kinds of calories to fuel my workouts. I probably shouldn't have had the fries, but I couldn't say no." Same.

"How much do you work out per day?" I knew I was firing a lot of questions at her, but I was fascinated. I wanted to know how her body came to look like that. What did it take to carve out those muscles?

"Depends on the day. And CrossFit isn't necessarily about working out longer, it's about doing high-intensity movements. Instead of lifting twenty pounds a hundred times, lift sixty thirty times. There's a lot of rest in between as well." Huh. I had no idea. It had all seemed like a total white douche-bro kind of thing, but Tuesday definitely wasn't that.

She told me more about CrossFit, and I realized that this was the most she'd talked about something since we met. So she *could* talk about something. It was clear in the tone of her voice and the way she used her hands that she loved what she was talking about. I imagined that I looked a little bit like that when I talked about yoga.

Tuesday paused and her face went a little red.

"Sorry," she said, and I watched her retreat into herself again.

"What for? I asked. I wanted to know." She sighed and the waiter brought the check. Before I could reach for it, she snapped it up.

"I've got this," she said. Not that I wanted to pay for all she'd eaten, but I was a little insulted that she hadn't even given me a chance to ask to split it. I could have just paid for my own stuff.

"Fine," I said, gritting my teeth.

"You wanna pay for all my shit?" she asked, sliding her card into the slot and putting it on the table with a crack.

"No, but I would have split it. This isn't a date." For the first time, I actually heard her laugh. It was a low sound that reverberated through my body and made my blood concentrate in interesting areas. I shivered a little. I rubbed my hands up and down my arms. They'd broken out in goosebumps.

"No, this isn't a date," she agreed, shaking her head. She didn't make any other comments about it or say something like "no homo," so I took that as a good sign. You could never tell when someone was going to come out as a raging bigot, so I was always wary when it came to new people until I had confirmation otherwise. So far so good with Tuesday.

We left the café and went back to our building. I guess it was technically *her* building. I didn't like that she had so much power over me. Sure, I had a lease, but she could still make my life miserable if she wanted to.

"Thanks for lunch," I said, as we paused in front of the gym door.

"Thanks for helping me with the logo," she said. I wasn't sure what else to say, but I had to get upstairs to make sure I had time to check everyone in for class.

"Sorry, I have to go," I said. I wasn't sure why I was apologizing. We were clearly done here.

"Have fun," she said, and pushed through the door. That was that.

Chapter Four

A FEW HOURS LATER, it started again. That music. I was right in the middle of a sun salutation, and there it was. If possible, it was louder than ever. I had to bite my tongue so I didn't curse right as my students were going into downward-facing dog. My jaw locked up, and it was a struggle to keep my voice level as I took them through the rest of the flow and onward to savasana.

I thought Tuesday and I had made progress, but I guess not. Now I was being punished for . . . having lunch with her? What the fuck was this shit? A few people made comments about the music and I tried to be as diplomatic as possible, but if this continued, I would not be responsible for my actions. As soon as everyone was out of the studio, I let out a primal scream.

"Everything okay?" said a voice behind me, and I spun around. Ellen was there, leaning on her walker and smirking.

"Yup, fine." I pointed to the floor where the vibrations from the music were tickling my feet something terrible, "except for THAT."

"Yeah, what is up with the music? You'd think the floors or ceilings would be thicker, but this is an old building and I guess not? It's pretty bad."

"I know," I said. "I've talked to her about it, but it's like this weird game to her." This wasn't a game to me, and I was pissed that she was interfering with my business.

"Who is her?" Ellen asked.

"Oh, our new landlord, Tuesday. She owns the gym downstairs and is responsible for that." I jabbed my finger at the floor again. "*She* apparently has a vendetta against me. I thought the endless construction down there was going to be there worst, but no, this is like slow torture."

"Torture by tunes," Ellen said.

"Exactly."

"So what are you going to do about it?" she asked.

I threw up my hands. "I don't know what else to do. I've been down there already, but it's not working. I literally just had lunch with her; I don't know why she's doing this." Ellen tilted her head to the side. I couldn't get over how cute her hair looked with her freckles. Just so adorable. Both her girlfriends were so lucky.

"I have a theory, but you're not ready to hear it," she said, and started to leave. I grabbed the mop and started working on cleaning the floor.

"It better not be that she has a crush on me!" I called after her, but she just waved and hit the button for the elevator.

"See you tomorrow," she said, as the doors opened.

"Bye," I called, and then it was just me and the mop and the music. That motherfucking music. I turned on some yoga chants, but it couldn't do anything in the presence of such an intense stereo. I didn't turn the music up too loud during class, since it could be distracting when you were trying to get into a good mental place. Now I was wishing I'd put in some massive concert-style speakers so I could blast Tuesday away.

I wasn't going to go down there and yell at her again. That hadn't worked last time. I was going to try something different: ignore her. I wasn't sure how long I could last, but I was going to try. If I could go on a silent retreat and not speak for a week, I could ignore this shit for a few hours.

I puttered around the studio and hummed to myself, but after an hour it wormed its way into my brain and I couldn't shake it. I was going to be hearing base echoes when I went home.

So much for trying to ignore it.

Yet again, I stormed down the stairs and slammed the door open. Tuesday was alone again, lifting weights in the shortest shorts that could barely pass for shorts and a white and gray sports bra. Her back was coated with sweat and I could hear her breathing, even over the intense loudness of the music.

It took me a second to remember what I was going to say in the face of . . . all of that.

Tuesday finished lifting her set and dropped the weight bar with a clang. She reached for a towel and then turned around.

"Hey," she said. "Would you mind handing me that water bottle?" I narrowed my eyes.

"Turn. The. Music. Down. I thought we'd been over this before. I thought going to lunch with you was somehow going to change things, but no. You're still an asshole." I hadn't really meant to call her an asshole out loud, but something about her just slammed my rage button. To be completely honest, Tuesday hit a lot of my buttons.

"Ouch," she said, pretending to wince. "Did you really think we were BFFs now?" Her tone was harsh and sarcastic, and I couldn't believe this was the same person I'd just argued about the merits of ketchup with a few hours ago. "I didn't make you a friendship bracelet or anything, should I have? Do you want to come sleep over at my house? We can do prank calls and have pillow fights." My rage-o-meter was off the charts at this point.

"Now you're mocking me *and* being a complete asshole. Also, prank calls are mostly impossible since everyone has caller ID on their phones. Unless you've got a burner phone or use a third-party service to make it." Her eyebrows went up a little.

"You have a lot of knowledge about prank calls?"

I waved that off.

"That isn't the point. You're being a dick, and I want it to stop. Either cut it out, or install some soundproofing in this place. My students are getting upset and so help me, if this messes with my business, I will make your life a fucking hell. I don't care if you're my landlord." I hadn't noticed that I'd walked toward her until I was right up in her face. My body shook a little, and hot and cold flashes rolled through me. I had to look up a little to meet those cold blue eyes, but I found something else in them that I couldn't read. They snapped with a fire that was like lightning.

"What are you going to do about it?"

I hadn't noticed before, but she had really long eyelashes. They looked fake, but I bet they weren't. She also had a tiny brown fleck in her left eye. Like a freckle.

That wasn't relevant.

My chest heaved as I breathed hard, and I didn't know what to do, I just knew I had to do *something*. The air sizzled between us. Her lips parted just a little. I stared at her mouth for a little too long.

Instead of shoving her (which wouldn't work, and would

probably end badly for me), or doing anything else that I might regret, I stomped over to the stereo and flipped it off.

"That's what I'm going to do," I said and then stormed out. She didn't call after me, but the music didn't come on for the rest of the day.

∽

"I DON'T KNOW what to do, Zee," I said that night. We were on the couch with pizza again. I had both kitties in my lap, and one of my best comfort movies on the TV. Zee was playing with my hair, putting little braids in it.

"I don't either. I mean, you're kind of stuck since she's your landlord. She can do what she wants, and you don't have a ton of recourse."

"I'm half-tempted to order a bunch of soundproofing stuff and have it delivered there. I would, if I had any extra money." I sighed and shoved another bite of pizza in my mouth. Tomorrow night was the intermediate class I had dared Tuesday to come to. I had no idea if she would show up, and if she did, what she would do. Maybe she'd bring her own music.

"She did keep it off after you went down there, though, right?" Zee asked, shoving another garlic knot in their mouth. I'd also ordered mozzarella sticks. I had needed *all* the comfort foods tonight.

"Yeah, but for how long? I don't want to have to do that every single day forever. Maybe I should start looking at other studio spaces." The problem with that was that I didn't have the money to move, I didn't want to move, and I liked my studio where it was. Changing the location would mean I basically had to start over. I was not fucking doing that.

"Is there anything you can do to retaliate?" I shook my head.

"I mean, nothing that I could think of. I don't want to start a war. I just want her to be less of a dick." I also wanted her to be less attractive. I had shivers from seeing her working out the second time. I'd never seen a body move like hers. It was like a brutal dance.

"I'm not sure she's going to do that, but maybe don't go to lunch with her anymore." Yeah, I wouldn't be making that mistake again. I'd thought we had gotten somewhere, made some progress. Then she was back on her bullshit a few hours later. What was *wrong* with her? Did she just enjoy making me angry? What kind of person did that?

It was a mystery that I wasn't going to waste my time on. I'd just go down and turn down the music from now on. Maybe I wouldn't even speak to her. Just go in and do it and walk out. See how she liked that.

∽

ONE OF MY OTHER TEACHERS, Priya, was teaching the Tuesday morning class so I didn't have to go in so early, which was amazing. Still, I woke up at six-thirty because I woke up at that time every day, and not by choice. I went out to the kitchen and found Zee making breakfast. We did our little routine of me asking if I could help, and them saying no, and me grumpily drinking my coffee until breakfast was ready.

I ate and then went back to bed for a little while and messed on my phone. I purposely did not look up anything about Tuesday. It was difficult, but I kept my fingers from typing out her name.

Too itchy to stay at home, I said goodbye to the kitties and headed over to the studio. Fortunately for me, it wasn't too far from my apartment and had decent parking, a rarity in Boston.

I noticed a car that I'd seen a few times in the lot and I

wondered if it belonged to Tuesday. I didn't know what time she came in every day, but I just had the feeling that car was hers. I also had the feeling that I should let some air out of her tires, but I didn't want to get arrested and there were security cameras, so I walked on by.

"What are you doing here?" Priya said when I came up the stairs. Her class had just gotten out and the lobby area was packed with sweaty people gathering their things and wandering around. Yoga brain was a real thing and it could cause you to forget just about anything after class. I'd seen people almost fall down the stairs because they were in such a daze.

"What are you talking about? I'm always here," I said, rolling my eyes. A few of my regular students stopped to say hello and I asked them about life updates and how their kids were and how the new job was going and how their bird of paradise pose was coming along. That took much longer than I thought it would, and by the time I made it into my office in the back, it was over an hour later.

I didn't hear any music. I was completely attuned to any kind of noise now. The second I heard anything, I was going to go downstairs, walking in, and turning it off. This was my new strategy. I hoped I wouldn't need it.

The rest of the day I taught two classes and worked on some paperwork and social media and the other minutia that were involved in running a business that never seemed to get done.

At last, it was time to prepare for my intermediate class. Part of me considered going downstairs to remind Tuesday that I'd dare her. Another part of me knew that she wasn't going to forget. She'd seemed pretty serious about the dare. A third part of me couldn't wait to see her completely struggle and tell me that I was right, and yoga was hard. I was going to wear the biggest smirk when that happened, and that victory was going to sustain me for a long time. The next time the music came on, I was going to rub her face in it. So satisfying.

I wasn't normally a petty person, but Tuesday knew how to get to me. I just wanted to return the favor. It was only fair.

As the time drew closer for the class and people started arriving, I wondered if she would show. If she didn't, I would have backing down on her dare to shove in her face too, so I was just winning all around. I smiled to myself.

Then I saw a dark head of hair coming up the stairs, her lips pressed into a grim line as if she was being marched to war or going to the RMV.

Before I could say anything, she put her hand up to stop me.

"I'm just doing this as a dare. This doesn't mean I think yoga is a thing." I wanted to argue with her on that point, but I nodded instead.

"Do you need to rent a mat?" She gave me a look.

"Do I have to?"

"To participate in the class, yes, you have to have a mat. And you're probably going to want a towel and some water as well." Tuesday groaned like I was asking her to do her taxes or something.

"Fine," she said. "Whatever."

I couldn't help but find some satisfaction in how uncomfortable and miserable she seemed. People came in around her and gave her looks that she returned as glares. I hoped she didn't throw off the vibe in the room, because that was really important. My yogis didn't need to have someone messing with their practice and sending out bad energy.

Tuesday hung around in the lobby until it was nearly time to go in. I had a rush of people and couldn't hold her hand, but I expected her to just take her mat and go in, but she didn't seem like she wanted to.

"Ready?" I asked as I checked the last person in and looked at the clock. Showtime.

"No," she said, but followed me in. I set her up near the front, but away from most of the other people. The class was a little bit smaller since it was mostly my dedicated yogis who wanted to challenge themselves and work on some of the more difficult poses like handstands and inversions. They tended to cluster together on one side of the room for some reason.

I opened class with everyone chanting 'om' once. I kept one eye on Tuesday and noticed she wasn't chanting with everyone else. Nothing shocking there. She pretty much had one eyebrow permanently raised. I started the music and began with going through a sun salutation slowly once.

Tuesday seemed to catch on, but she was doing some of the moves a little clumsily, so I went over and gave her a few pointers and was treated to a murderous glare as thanks, but her downward-facing dog improved, so who was the real winner?

We moved from the warmup into balancing poses and I had to correct Tuesday again, but she was doing well for a newbie. She'd already broken a sweat and I could see her muscles shaking a bit. Instead of taking the beginner poses, she went right for the more advanced ones that she definitely wasn't ready for. She did a lot of tipping over and I had to try not to laugh. Yeah, she was getting her ass kicked. Doing the poses right was not the point of yoga, at all, but still. I got quite the satisfaction from seeing her not have an easy time of it.

Then we moved to the inversions and she did great on holding a handstand, but not so much on trying handstand splits. Her forearm stand was also impressive, so I had to give credit where credit was due.

We finished with some backbends and ab work and she collapsed halfway through the backbends. I wanted to cheer.

When I walked around the room when everyone was in savasana, I tried not to stare and gloat at her, but she was completely drenched and lying there like she'd died.

I ended the class with one final chant of 'om,' and she didn't participate in that one either. The other students cleaned their mats and chatted and had water and gathered their things. Tuesday sat on her mat, still breathing a little hard. Once everyone else had left, she was the only one in the room, sitting there and staring at the wall.

"So," I said, sinking down to the floor and crossing my legs. "How did it go?" It took all of my willpower not to smirk at her. I was so glad that she'd taken this dare.

"Don't talk to me," Tuesday said, her eyes opening only a little until they were little slits. I'd never been glared at quite like that.

"You ready to admit that yoga is harder than you thought it was? That's it's not just a bunch of fancy stretching that anyone can do?" Tuesday closed her eyes again.

"Never," she said. "Just wait until you try CrossFit. This is *nothing* compared to that." I thought about scoffing myself and saying that I would rather be hit by a truck than do CrossFit.

Instead I said, "Do you dare me?"

Her eyes opened all the way in surprise.

"You don't seem like a dare kind of girl." She used her towel to wipe her face and I tried not to focus on the sweat that trickled down her chest and disappeared into her sports bra.

"You don't know anything about me, Tuesday," I said. She really didn't. We'd barely spent any time together.

"Is that a no?" she said, stretching her legs out in front of her and then crossing them at the ankles with a wince. I savored that wince like a glass of wine after a long day.

"Okay, Tuesday. I'll come to your gym when it opens. I'm not working out in there alone with just you. That would be weird." I didn't think I could handle having her watch me struggle to lift weights and do whatever else they did in CrossFit. Flipping tires? Hauling dead bodies? I wasn't really sure what it entailed. Guess I was going to find out.

"It's a dare," she said, sticking out her hand.

"Are we supposed to shake to confirm dares?" I asked.

"Yes." I put my hand in hers and was expecting her to squeeze it so hard my fingers would ache, but she didn't. The handshake was firm and a little sweaty. She looked into my eyes and I had simultaneous urges to lean closer and run away. I'd never met someone I'd been so conflicted about in my life. I dropped her hand and stood up.

"So, you ready to do a trial membership?" I asked, backing away from her and going to get the mop to clean the floor.

"You're gonna charge me?" she asked, grabbing some wipes to clean off the mat.

"Yeah, I'm not doing this for free. Not in this economy." I needed every single cent I could get to keep my head above water. She should know that, as an owner herself.

"Fair enough," she said. "I'll think about it." She rolled up the now clean mat and handed it to me.

"Towels go in the hamper," I said, pointing to the corner of the room. She walked the towel over and I got to watch her ass *and* see her moving a little slow. Ha. If she was sore now, she was going to be miserable in two days.

It was getting late and I was starving, but Tuesday didn't seem to want to leave. She lingered as I wiped down the floors and turned off the heat and cut off the music.

"What are your plans tonight?" I asked, because I couldn't deal with the silence. I'd always been a little awkward in these kinds of situations and it seemed like Tuesday brought all those tendencies to the forefront.

"Going home, feeding my turtles. Eating. I spend a lot of time eating." That did not surprise me. What did surprise me was the second thing.

"Turtles? You really have turtles?" She'd mentioned them before, and I thought she was joking. Her face was still a little red from the class, but I swear it got a little brighter, as if she hadn't meant to admit that. Yoga brain was real. Sometimes it was almost like being drunk.

"Never mind," she muttered and left the room. I put the mop away and followed her out to the lobby.

"No, tell me about the turtles," I said. I'd always wanted turtles, but my parents wouldn't allow me to have pets (other than my one outdoor cat) because there was no one home to take care of them. We were always at one of their businesses. I'd spent more time sleeping at the restaurant and under the desk of the computer shop than in my own bed when I was younger. I'd longed for a dog, but the answer had always been no. My apartment didn't allow dogs, and I was at the studio too much now, so that still wasn't an option. Someday. Someday I was going to have two French bulldogs and I was going to spoil them rotten.

Tuesday ducked her head and shuffled her feet and it hit me square in the chest. She was so tough and so strong, but she was also so completely adorable in this moment.

"Do they have names? Tell me about the turtles. I'll show you pictures of my kittens." I grabbed my phone and started scrolling through it and found one of the kittens asleep on Zee's chest.

"Tell me about the turtles and I'll show you the kittens. You know you want to see the kittens." She pressed her lips together, as if she was trying to hold back a smile and failing.

"Fine," she said, and fished her phone out of a secret pocket in her shorts. "Their names are Mary and Percy Shelley." I grinned at her.

"Really? Those are such great turtle names. Can I see them?" She pulled up a few videos on her phone of two little red-eared sliders happily swimming in a huge tank.

"Aw, they're cute. These are my babies. Mocha and Cappuccino." I showed her several pictures of the kittens and her face softened, just a little.

"I'm only allowed to have a pet that can live in an aquarium in my apartment, so I went with turtles. They're not the most conventional pets, but I love those little fuckers." The love in her voice was there and I softened a little bit toward Tuesday. It was hard to be enraged at someone who showed you pictures of their turtles.

"I should get going," she said, putting her phone away. "I need to shower, bad."

"We have showers," I suggested.

"That's fine. I've got my own downstairs. I'll, uh, see you later." She ran away before I could say anything else. Why was she always doing that? It was like anytime I got anywhere close to knowing anything personal about her, she couldn't handle it so she bolted. Interesting.

Interesting and frustrating. I still didn't know if I liked her, or if I wanted to know why she shied away from anything personal. I definitely liked looking at her body. There was so much to look at and it was so, so gorgeous. She'd worked so hard for it, the least I could do was appreciate her. Props to Tuesday on her fitness.

After she left, I gathered my stuff and headed to my car. My stomach was weak from hunger and I hoped there were leftovers at home that Zee had made.

"You're so late, did you fall asleep doing payroll again?"

Zee asked when I walked into the house. They were in the kitchen and there was a pot of something that smelled of tomatoes and garlic and spices bubbling on the stove. My wish had been granted.

The babies cried and cried until I picked them up and danced them through the kitchen.

"No. Tuesday came to class." Zee turned around and their eyes went wide.

"Tell me everything," they said, pointing at me with a wooden spoon and splattering whatever they were cooking on the floor. I put down the kitties and cleaned up the mess before I answered.

"So, she survived, but barely. She could do some of the inversions, but she couldn't hold them. The look on her face at the end was priceless. Totally worth it. But," I said, taking a dramatic pause, "I agreed to do CrossFit on a dare. I might die. Start planning my funeral. I'd like to be cremated and my ashes spread at the Grand Canyon." Zee stirred the pot and I peeked in and found their chili. Instantly, my mouth started watering. Zee made the best chili. They made the best everything, but their chili was world class.

"Cremated, got it," they said, adding another pinch of salt to the pot before tossing a little bit over their shoulder.

"Seriously, I have no idea what I'm doing. I said I wouldn't go until the gym opened, but that's happening sooner rather than later." What had I agreed to? The kittens cried at my feet as if they were dying so I picked them up again.

"Mommy is going to die doing CrossFit. What do you think about that?" Cappy licked my nose and Mocha yawned.

"Thanks for your concern."

I didn't tell Zee about the turtles for some reason. It wasn't like it was some shameful secret, but Tuesday had been so cute about it. I didn't think someone who looked like her could be considered *cute*, but it was true.

Tuesday was cute and sexy and surly and seductive and so many things, but she was still a total mystery. One that I wasn't sure if I wanted to be the one to solve.

Chapter Five

I DIDN'T HAVE any interaction with Tuesday for the rest of the week. Things were quiet at work, except I kept finding packages meant for downstairs in front of the door to my studio. I sighed and walked them downstairs and put them in front of the gym door. I'd thought it was a fluke on the first day, but then it kept happening. What was wrong with the delivery guys? Some of the packages were so heavy, I just kicked them down the stairs because there was no way I was breaking my back for her crap.

The weekend came and I decided I needed to do something social outside the yoga studio. Over the past few years I'd gotten into a rut of spending too much time at the studio and then coming home and not doing anything that didn't involve work or sleep. Zee forced me to do social things at least twice a month, which was good for both of us.

I'd arranged drinks and dinner with Zee, Ellen, John, and Celia. Dan and Mischa were away together, so they couldn't come, but we looped them in on our group chat, so it was like they were there anyway. Ellen's girlfriends Tatiana and

Carmen were home because Tati was sick and Carmen was playing nurse. So sweet, but I still missed them.

Zee and I were the first ones to show up, so we ordered drinks and started looking at the menu, not that we needed to. We'd been to this place so many times they knew our drink orders without us having to ask. I'd decided to try something new and got their special mojito. Zee was fancy and got a dirty martini, as usual.

John and Celia were next, coming in together, their hands entwined. Celia had on her heels, and even without them was at least four inches taller than John.

The two of them had been friends forever and had only started dating in the past few months. It was still a jolt to see them behaving in romantic ways, but I was thrilled. They were perfect for each other. I greeted them with hugs and then Ellen walked in with her cane and completed the group.

"Love the hair," John said, pointing to Ellen's head. She'd done it up tonight in a bunch of braids and looked like she belonged at a Renaissance Faire.

"Thanks, it was time for a change. I hadn't tried orange yet."

"It suits you," Celia said, leaning on John's shoulder. My heart fluttered a little and I wasn't going to say it was jealousy, but it was a distant relative of jealousy.

The rest of the group ordered drinks and we all caught up. A warm feeling flowed through my body, and it wasn't just the result of the alcohol.

"Any updates on the landlord?" Celia asked. They all knew about Tuesday via our group chat. I hadn't told them everything, but they'd figured out enough. Except for the fact that I'd been having dreams about licking every single muscle on Tuesday's body to figure out if they tasted different. That one I was keeping to myself.

"Nope, haven't seen her in a few days. No idea what she's doing. The music hasn't been an issue, but they keep delivering heavy packages for her upstairs and it's seriously annoying. I wish I could go back in time and save the building from being sold."

"Hmmm," Ellen said, sipping her gin and tonic.

"What?" I asked, even though I was afraid to ask.

"I have a theory, but I'm not going to tell you what it is. I'm going to see how things play out." She smirked at me and I glared back.

"Ohhhh, can you tell me the theory?" Celia said, leaning over to Ellen.

"Nope, I'm going to keep this one to myself."

"This is really annoying, you know," I said, but Ellen just laughed.

"We'll see. I could be totally wrong." Ellen wasn't wrong a lot, in my experience.

Eager to change the subject, I asked John about his job. All of our phones sounded off with notifications from Dan and Mischa asking for updates.

"We should just video-chat them in. I don't know why we don't just do that," I said, typing out a quick response.

Our food arrived and the drinks flowed and I was relieved to not be thinking about Tuesday for once. Okay, that was a lie. I was still thinking about her. Every time I saw a person with long dark hair, my body jolted, as if the person was going to turn around and be Tuesday. The chances of her being in this place were beyond slim, but that didn't stop me from jumping every time.

Celia messed with Ellen's hair, asking if she should dye hers orange. John said no in the most polite way. Orange wouldn't be a good color on Celia.

"It wouldn't enhance your beauty," John said, and we all let out a chorus of "aww" at that. He really was a charmer. He was cute as hell with glasses and a crooked smile. If I liked guys at all, John would be the kind of guy I'd have a crush on, no doubt.

"Nice, John," Celia said, kissing him on the cheek. "I know you're just partial to my current hair color." Celia's hair was naturally dark brown with incredible red highlights in the sun and hung almost to her waist. Hell, *I* was jealous of it. My hair was an uninteresting dark blonde verging on brown naturally and I enhanced it with highlights so it wasn't so blah.

"I'm partial to everything about you," John said, and we all made noises again.

"Stop it, you're being gross," Celia said, but she smiled so hard I thought her face was going to break.

"You're just making me want to go home to my girls," Ellen said, picking up her phone to send a message to said girls.

"How's Tati?" I asked. She had an autoimmune disease and a lot of food allergies, so getting sick for her wasn't just a run-of-the-mill cold.

"She's pissed she couldn't come, so you all better send her messages and funny pictures," Ellen said, glaring at everyone.

"On it," I said, sending her three pictures of the kittens. She sent me back kissy face emojis. Zee made a face next to me and took a picture to send to Tati saying that we missed her and we'd see her soon.

"Should we drop by maybe on Sunday?" I asked Ellen.

"Let me see how she's doing and I'll let you know."

I made a note to pick up some of her favorite cookies so even if we couldn't hang out, I could at least drop something off.

We ended the night with sharing desserts and laughing way too loudly and getting looks from the other people in the restaurant. We didn't care, and kept going even though we'd all talked about leaving for at least an hour.

Zee and I ordered a car to go home and gave everyone tons of hugs and promises that we needed to do this more often than we did, and reminding each other of our upcoming plans for John's birthday. Originally it was going to be a surprise party, but surprises made John anxious, so we'd scrapped that idea and had let him pick the time and place for his party.

When we got home, I snuggled into bed with the kittens and let my tipsy mind drift. Of course, my brain drifted right to thinking about Tuesday. It was doing that more and more, especially since I hadn't seen her. What was she doing? Was she away? Had something happened? I didn't want to go into a panic scenario because what if she was just busy with something else?

I was being ridiculous. Fueled by the alcohol, I pulled up her social media pages on my phone, looking for clues. Nothing. I would have had to add her as a friend to view most of them, and I wasn't going to do that. Instead I just scrolled through all the other photos of her I could find online. Again. Every time I saw her face with those eyes my stomach flipped over and over, like it was in the circus.

I needed to stop this, but I couldn't.

"Help me," I said to the sleeping kittens. They just kept sleeping. A lot of help they were.

"I have a problem," I said to myself. A Tuesday problem, every day of the week.

Then I did something reckless and ridiculous: I requested to be her friend or follower on every single one of her social pages. My eyes closed and I fell asleep before I could see if she'd accepted me.

THE FIRST SOUND I made the next morning was a moan. I hadn't had that much to drink in a while, and I was feeling it today. Why had I done that? I remembered everything that happened last night, but it was a little hazy. I'd woken up with my face smashed into my phone, which hadn't been charging so it was dead.

I didn't want to move, but I also needed something fried and some caffeine right the fuck now, and I could hear sounds in the kitchen. Zee was awake and cooking. What would I do without them?

"Hey," I croaked at them with a little wave as I shuffled into the kitchen.

"You look rough, here," they said, pressing a cup of coffee into my hands. "Bacon and cheese sandwiches are on the way. You're lucky I had some croissants left over to put them on." That sounded amazing right now. I sipped the purely black coffee and groaned again. My stomach was not impressed with me. I would have to be careful not to give it too much too fast. This was a delicate balance.

"That was fun last night," I said, my voice still rough. I'd also talked a lot and loudly, because my friends tended to be high volume.

"Yeah, I'm glad you didn't cancel like last time." They glared at me before carefully flipping the bacon over so it crisped on both sides.

"Hey, I had a workshop and I had to be there." Sure, I could have had my other teacher, Priya, stay, but I'd wanted to be there and be the face of the studio. I couldn't let go of that, and I didn't know if I ever would. The studio had grown enough that I could probably step back a little from all the teaching and managing and maybe hire an extra teacher or a studio manager, but I just couldn't let go. I'd worked so fucking hard and I didn't want to lose what I'd built, or for it to get screwed up by someone else doing something wrong.

"You really need to hire another teacher. Or two, at least. You've had so many people ask." It was true, I'd had lots of yoga teachers wanting to come and work at Breathe, but I hadn't done anything about it yet.

"I know, I know," I mumbled, as I waited for the sandwiches to be ready. I didn't start to feel better until the coffee kicked in and I was halfway through my first croissant sandwich.

"I should have made some home fries, but I figured they would take too long and you needed food in your system quicker than that." They were right, if I'd waited much longer for food, I probably would have thrown up.

My phone made a bunch of noises in my bedroom and I got up to see what was happening.

"Oh no. Oh nononono," I said when I saw my notifications.

"What? What happened?" Zee was instantly at my side.

"I did something bad. I followed and friended Tuesday in a fit of ridiculousness fueled by alcohol last night. I knew I'd done something before I fell asleep, but I couldn't remember what it was. Oh, crap." Great, now I was going to have to deal with this.

"Looks like she accepted all your requests, though," Zee said, pointing to the notifications that said Tuesday had accepted me.

And she'd sent me a message on each of them.

"I feel like I'm dying," I said, putting my hand on my chest and then sinking back onto the couch. The kitties meowed and seemed concerned.

"It's okay, my loves. Your momma just did something silly." Zee picked them both up and cradled them in their arms.

"She sent me a bunch of messages. I don't know if I'm up for reading them. I might need another drink." I needed to get to work soon, but there was a chance that I'd see Tuesday there, so should I just deal with this right now?

"I'm sure it's fine. Just do it. You've got this." I took a huge breath before I opened the first message.

How's it going, stalker?

I rolled my eyes. Whatever. I moved to the second.

Wow, you're really going for it. You wanna be my friend, Sutton?

I swear, I read the message in her voice.

I flipped through the other messages and they were all variations on the same theme. Except for the last:

What's a girl like you doing on a site like this in the middle of the night? Are you in bed, thinking about me?

"Well?" Zee said. They'd been waiting to hear what the messages were. I'd expected them to stand and read over my shoulder, but they didn't.

"It's nothing," I said, locking my phone. I wasn't going to respond to those messages. At least not until I had the sharpest, wittiest comeback that would slice Tuesday to ribbons and make sure that she never messaged me again.

"Is it?" they said, a sly smile on their face.

"Yes, it's *nothing*," I said with emphasis. I grabbed Mocha from them and rubbed my face in her belly. "What are your plans today?" Most days I was jealous of their nine-to-five job, but then I remembered that I was my own boss, so it was a tradeoff.

"Gym, library, hanging out with all my other friends," they said. I pretended to glare.

"How dare you have friends that I don't know about." Zee gave me a kiss on the cheek and cackled.

"It's okay, of all my friends, you're my bestest." I wiped an imaginary tear from my eye.

"Same, Zee, same. I'll never have a friend like you. Never, ever." We put the kittens down and hugged it out, laughing.

"No, really, I'm having lunch with a friend from work. That's it. She's going through a rough time." I waved them off.

"You don't have to explain. I'm just mad I have to work on the weekends." Zee rolled their eyes. "But I am going to stop and see Tati, or at least drop off some cookies for her before I go in."

"You know, you could fix that. Just hire teachers for those classes and then you can have a weekend just like me." They had a point. I'd always refused to consider doing that before, but I was tired. I was getting burned out. I wanted to do things other than just live at the studio and think about budgets and inventory and membership reports all the time.

"I don't know," I said.

"Listen, you've got this. You can let go of some of the control. Just hire someone you trust. You've done that twice before and you can do it again. They'll do what you want because you'll train them and be on their ass all the time." They were making a lot of sense.

"I'll think about it," I said. "I only promise to think about it. And maybe run some calculations." The other thing I wanted to do was open up my own teacher-training program. That would be a huge commitment and I'd definitely need tons of help for that, so I definitely wasn't ready. Someday. I'd get there.

"Good." I got ready for work and then drove to the store to grab the cookies. I left them with Carmen, who said that Tati was still not doing well, but I asked her to give Tatiana a kiss for me. I didn't see what I thought was Tuesday's car when I got to the studio and breathed a sigh of relief. Where had she been this week? I was almost tempted to ask her. Instead, I pulled up one of her pages and looked through her pictures.

There were the turtles, featured prominently. On Halloween she even put little hats on them. Her most recent picture was from yesterday and it was a picture of her lifting a barbell over her head. She must have had someone else take it. From her surroundings it looked like another gym, not the one she was building. The walls were gray instead of white.

I went through a few other videos. Well. Tuesday could certainly lift a lot of weight and do a lot of handstand walks. My mouth started watering and I closed the page on my phone. I realized that I'd been standing in the parking lot for nearly twenty minutes and I needed to get my ass upstairs and heat up the room because I was teaching soon.

Tuesday was a distraction that I didn't need, now or ever. I had other shit in my life. She was just a complication. A sexy and irritating as hell complication.

Chapter Six

The packages were piled in front of the door on Monday morning and the music was on. I hadn't seen anything more from Tuesday all weekend, and I'd somehow stayed away from her social pages, but only through tremendous willpower.

Since the music was on, I figured she was there, so I turned around and headed back down the stairs. I pushed the door open and found her arranging some t-shirts on racks.

"Seriously?" I asked, gesturing at the speakers.

"Good morning to you too," she said, not pausing what she was doing.

"And you need to figure out why your shit keeps ending up in front of my door. It's heavy and I don't feel like lugging it back down here. I have a class coming in a few minutes." She finally stopped and turned around.

"So, yoga doesn't make you that strong if you can't handle a few boxes." All of the goodwill she'd earned was gone.

"You," I said, pointing my finger at her. I couldn't think of what to call her, I was so steamed.

"Me," she said, a smirk ghosting on her lips. Oh, she enjoyed this far too much. The victory of her being crushed by yoga was merely a memory now. I wanted her to take a flexibility workshop and have her ass completely kicked again.

"You are just . . ." I still couldn't come up with something. Tuesday stepped so close to me I gasped.

"I'm what, Sutton?" Hearing my name from her lips did something strange to me. I'd never reacted this way to my own name before. I'd heard it probably millions of times, but hearing Tuesday saying it was like hearing it for the first time. Having her so close sucked all the air out of my lungs.

"What am I?" she said, her voice soft for the first time. I didn't know what she was. I didn't know what I was. I didn't know what *anything* was at the moment. Except that I didn't know how to make my lungs work anymore.

I stumbled backward right into the new desk that hadn't been there before. Before I could fall into the furniture and completely wipe out, Tuesday reached for my arm and kept me upright.

"Careful there, princess." I wanted to bristle at the nickname because I definitely wasn't a princess, but I was too busy trying to keep my feet under me and not fall over again.

"Just get your shit away from my door," I said, my voice trembling a little. Time to go.

"I'll see what I can do," she said, as the door shut behind me. I had to step over the boxes to get to the door to open the studio up, and I kept periodically checking to see if they had moved. No progress, and it was twenty minutes before my next class and I was not going to have my students stepping over fucking boxes to get to yoga. That was a hazard and it was also ridiculous. Ready to storm downstairs, I looked out again and the boxes were gone. The music also went down a few seconds later. That wasn't so hard, was it?

I relaxed and everything went back to normal by the time my first student arrived.

My mind kept drifting while I was teaching. I'd done enough classes that if I didn't need to be present, I could check out a little bit and still look like I was completely in the moment. Not the best idea, but sometimes you needed a mental break after teaching so many classes in a week. It was more draining than people knew.

Tuesday. What was her deal? She hadn't mentioned anything about the social pages and the midnight following, and I hadn't commented back to her either. I didn't know what to do with that. I should just block her from everything, but that would lead to questions. Right now, my strategy was to ignore her. That could totally work, as long as she stopped pissing me off.

∾

THE PACKAGES WEREN'T in front of my door the next day, but I did notice that there was a new sign in front of the gym. It was opening in three weeks. My stomach plummeted into my feet. Three weeks and I'd have to try her class. She hadn't said anything about coming back to yoga, so I figured that was over, but it was Tuesday night again and I looked up to find her waiting there.

"Can I rent a mat?" she asked, and I couldn't read the expression on her face. She still didn't look thrilled to be here, but she was.

"You're taking class?" I asked. I hadn't charged her for last time because we offered our first class free, but now she'd have to pay for a drop in, or get a membership.

"Yeah, I figured I'd give it another shot," she said, and her eyes were so sharp, they dared me not to comment on any of it.

"Okay," I said, handing her a mat. "Do you want to just do the one class?"

"You're charging me?" she asked.

"Yeah. Why wouldn't I? I have rent to pay. To *you*." I hated that she was my landlord. It added an extra layer of complexity to this already stacked situation. Thinking about layers just made me think about lasagna. I made a mental note to get the ingredients on my way home and maybe Zee would make one later this week. I needed pasta and cheese and sauce ingredients and fresh basil. Zee made the best fucking pasta sauce in the entire world. I would fill a tub with that shit and bathe in it if I could.

"Fine," Tuesday said, pulling a card from her phone case and handing it over. "But I think I should get free classes."

"Your comment has been noted, I'll take it to the management," I said, swiping the card viciously.

"You're the management," Tuesday pointed out.

"I'll see what I can do," I said, giving her a sweet smile.

"Thanks," she mumbled, grabbing the card back from me and putting it away.

"You're welcome," I sang, and turned my attention to the next person. Tuesday stormed into the room and the door slammed behind her. People jumped and gave me looks.

"No idea," I said as an explanation. How did one explain Tuesday Grímsdóttir? I got everyone else checked in without incident and went into the room to teach. Everyone was stretched out on their mats, some with their eyes closed and breathing deep, getting their minds ready for class. Except Tuesday. She sat on the floor with her knees up and her arms draped on them, showing off her incredible arm muscles.

For a moment, I forgot who I was and what I was supposed to be doing. Like that feeling when you walked into a room and forgot why you went there in the first place. Tuesday's arms made it hard to think. I still didn't know exactly how much she could lift, but I was betting that she could pick me up without much effort. Why did that turn me on so much?

No lust in the studio, Sutton. Keep that in your yoga pants.

I cleared my throat and went to the front of the room to welcome everyone. Tuesday had her eyes on me and I pretended not to see her. It wasn't easy. Good thing I could teach this class on autopilot if I needed to, but I didn't want to. I had a new flow I wanted to try out after being inspired by something I'd seen online, and I'd even written down a few quotes that I wanted to share throughout the class to enhance the practice.

This time Tuesday didn't struggle as much with linking one move to the next. She knew what a forward fold was, she knew how to go from chaturanga to upward-facing dog without crashing her body onto the mat. One thing I could say for Tuesday: she learned quickly. Most students took at least three or more classes to be really comfortable with the moves, but here she was on her second class rocking it.

I sped things up a bit and mentioned some difficult variations that only a few people in the class could probably attempt. I didn't meet her eyes, but I hoped she knew I was challenging her.

She took the bait and fell out of a lot of poses. Tuesday wasn't as stable and flexible as she thought she was, and I did get a little satisfaction from that, but not much. At least there weren't fucking packages in front of my door.

She didn't chant at the end again, but whatever. This time she was quick to get up from her mat, clean it, and roll it back up. My attention was diverted by someone who didn't know this was hot yoga and was wondering why we kept it hot, and what the benefits of heat were. I figured she'd gone back downstairs until the studio emptied and I found her lurking in the doorway as I cleaned the floor.

"Still here?" I asked.

"It wasn't so bad this time. Guess I'm better at yoga than you thought." I finally got a full smirk from Tuesday and it was completely devastating. I had to hold onto the mop and use it to prop myself up so my knees didn't buckle.

If I ever got a real smile from Tuesday, it might completely end me. I started at her for a second and then she sighed and looked over her shoulder.

"I should probably get back downstairs. Lots to do before we open."

"Just make sure your shit doesn't end up in front of my door, thanks," I said, being a little snippier than I meant to. Whatever, she could take it and give it right back to me.

"Touchy," she commented. "I'll see what I can do." I made a little growling noise of frustration in my throat and she laughed as she went down the stairs.

I wanted to scream again.

∼

ZEE CAME to take me out for lunch on Wednesday because they had a rare day off.

Ellen had just taught a class, so she tagged along with us. She was having a good spine day so we all walked down the street to wait for the banh mi truck to get there. Zee had a tracker on their phone. Ellen sat on the little seat that attached to her walker and was busy on her phone.

"Stop sexting, it's rude," I said as a joke, but Ellen just grinned up at me.

"Wait, are you seriously sexting right now?" I asked, and she just shrugged.

"Gotta keep the romance alive." A little jolt of jealousy

went through me at that moment and I had to look away as she typed furiously on her phone.

A line formed before the truck even got there, but fortunately we were near the front. When the truck pulled in, everyone cheered. Well, almost everyone. Zee, Ellen, and I stayed quiet.

"I'll cheer when the food is in my hands," Zee said.

"Agreed," Ellen said.

We got our sandwiches and walked a little ways away to find a bench to sit on.

"I'm cheering on the inside," Zee said, through a mouthful of sandwich. I was also cheering on the inside. So many times I'd been disappointed by a banh mi that wasn't the real thing, but this was excellent.

"Thanks for getting me out of the studio," I said to Zee and they did a little bow.

"Thank you very much, sometimes I come in handy." I scoffed.

"You're *always* handy. Who was the one who fixed the sink, the dishwasher, and the toilet all in the same week?" Zee beamed.

"Yeah, that was me," they said.

"You wanna come over to my house? Tati refuses to hire anyone to fix things because she says she can do it herself, but then the things sort of get fixed, but not really? She gets so excited about it that Carm and I don't have the heart to do anything about it. So that's why everything in my house is taped together." That was so cute I could barely stand it.

"I would come over and fix everything and put the tape back so she didn't know, but I don't think I could deal with Tati's disappointment if she ever found out. It would be like kicking a puppy." Ellen nodded.

"So you see my problem."

We talked more about home repairs and relationships and jury duty and the latest streaming show everyone was obsessed with. It was a good break, and I'd needed it. In keeping my head down and working so hard, I'd neglected so many parts of myself that also needed to be nourished. I'd done the opposite of what I preached about in my yoga classes every day. Something about those who can't do, teach.

I dallied with Ellen and Zee until I definitely had to go back to the studio. Ellen came with me because she'd decided to take class. I got out her chair and made sure there were others in the back of the room for anyone who needed them.

"You okay?" I nodded.

"Yeah, just thinking about how I don't get away from this place and the business enough. I'm going to work more on that. Maybe cheat and take some yoga classes at another studio." I hadn't been practicing on the regular and that was something I absolutely needed in my life.

"I think that's a great idea. You need things in your life other than work. Perhaps a new hobby might be good. There's a gym opening up downstairs you know," she said with a grin.

"I'm not joining the gym," I said. Ellen knew about the dare, but I didn't want to fuel any kinds of speculation about what was going on between me and Tuesday, even though they were probably already speculating behind my back.

"We'll see," Ellen said in a singsong voice. "I'm going to get set up." She left me to handle check-in, but I wanted to run after her and reassure her that CrossFit would not be my new hobby. I'd rather take up stabbing myself in the face with knitting needles.

Irritated, I tried to get myself in a good headspace before class. I shut my office door and put on some music and did a quick meditation, but my mind wouldn't let go of my thoughts. They just keep sticking. I gave up and went to teach.

After I locked up for the night, I peered around to see if there were lights on in Tuesday's gym. There were. The door was open and she had fans going. The place looked a lot better. Now the walls had more decals on them; silhouettes of barbells and people doing squats and purple stars. Way better.

"You gonna keep staring or come in?" a voice said, and I gasped.

Tuesday came around the corner from where she'd been working on the retail area near the door.

"Sorry. I like the decals. They're a nice touch." I didn't know why I kept standing here, but I didn't want to leave. The building was quiet and I was exhausted from teaching classes all day. I needed food and kitten cuddles and bed. Maybe a sheet mask for good measure. And meditation. I needed that today as well.

"Thank you," she said, and I was shocked.

"How did you like your second class? We didn't really get to talk." I'd been too annoyed at her then.

"It was good. I'm not sure if I'm doing it right, but that doesn't matter, does it? It's all about the journey." Tuesday spoke in a somewhat mocking tone and I was quickly regretting stopping and talking to her.

"What is your problem with yoga? Seriously? You've been to two classes and I think you've gotten something out of it, but you keep shitting on it." Yoga meant so much to me and it hurt to have someone dismiss it like a bunch of silly movements and meaningless words.

"I just think that people overestimate the benefits and sell it as a cure. Depressed? Yoga. Sick? Yoga. Your house burned down? Yoga. It's ridiculous. Exercise is good, but it's not *that* good. You can't 'om' your way out of a shitty situation." I'd heard that before and I couldn't argue with her because she was right. Yoga had been packaged and monetized and turned into a commodity. It was also used as a bludgeon to throw at people who had real problems.

"You're right. But that doesn't mean yoga is bad. I have seen it change people's lives. No, it's not going to *cure* you of anything, but it can help you be more in touch with yourself and your body. It can help you be able to find that inner peace in moments of chaos. It's also about community. Some of my best friends have been made because of yoga. I'd think someone like you would understand that." I may or may not have done a quick skim of the official CrossFit site and that was one of the main pillars: community.

Tuesday rolled her eyes and sighed.

"I guess when you put it *that* way . . ."

"That's what I thought," I said, satisfied with myself. I turned around to leave, but then there was a warm hand on my shoulder.

"I'm sorry for insulting you. And insulting yoga," Tuesday said, and that somehow irritated me more.

"You didn't insult me, or yoga. And I'm not that fucking fragile, Tuesday." I turned around and met her eyes. Those icy eyes melted, just a little.

"Want to see a picture of the turtles?" she asked, and I almost burst out laughing.

"Yeah," I said. I definitely did. She pulled out her phone and showed me a video of them swimming and then one of them crawling on the floor and her cheering them on as they raced each other.

"You should sell tickets and make a bunch of money. Or livestream it." People would be all over that.

"I'm thinking of making them their own social pages," she said, scrolling through some more pictures. She had a ton.

"You should," I said. My irritation had evaporated at the mention of the turtles and I had the feeling she'd done that on purpose. The next time the music was up and she didn't turn it down, I hoped she didn't use the turtles to distract me.

"Is it just you here?" I asked. I hadn't seen any sort of business partner or anything.

"Yup, I'm a one-woman show. Didn't plan it that way, but shit happens. I'm still on track to open on time." Everything looked ready now, but I didn't know what else she still had to get in place.

"If you ever need any advice, I kind of know what I'm doing when it comes to running a business," I said. Wait, what? Had those words come out of my mouth? I was going to blame the turtles.

"Thanks, but I think I've got it," she snapped, and then softened a little.

"Sorry, I've had everyone and their uncle trying to tell me what to do and I'm fucking tired of it. I know you aren't saying that because you just want to tell me what to do."

"It's fine," I said. My stomach was screaming for food and I needed to get home to the kitties. Of course, Zee was with them, but I didn't want them to think that I wasn't ever coming back. That would wreck me.

"Listen, I need to get going, but I'll see you later?"

"Yeah, sounds good. I'm just going to order some pizza and eat it on the floor. Like I did last night." Bitter much?

I gave her a look and she groaned.

"It's been a long week and I'm tired and my filter is completely fucking gone. Leave before I get even nastier."

"I think I will." I left her with a little wave and then hurried out to the parking lot. Every interaction with Tuesday left me even more confused than ever. I was unlocking my car when I heard her voice again.

"Do you want some pizza?" She stood at the entrance to the building and had the door propped open with her body.

"What?" I'd been planning what I was going to have for dinner and figuring out what I had in the fridge, so it took me a second to understand what she'd said.

"Do you want some pizza?" I still couldn't read her face, but I thought she looked a little shy and wistful. Or maybe that was just the streetlights casting shadows that weren't actually there.

I wanted to get home, but something pulled me away from my car and made my lips form one word, "Sure." I threw my things in my car and locked it again.

Tuesday seemed unsure when I walked back into the building, but she didn't ask me if I was serious about doing this. I still didn't quite know what I was doing.

"Uh, what kind of pizza do you want? My treat," she said, pulling up an app to order.

"First of all, where are you ordering from?" I asked. Pizza was serious business to me, and I wasn't going to eat some second-rate crap, even if she was paying for it.

Tuesday mentioned the name and I made a face.

"Have you had it before?" I asked. She said that she hadn't.

"You don't want to order from there, trust me. It's a wonder that place hasn't gotten shut down by the health department yet. You want to order from Boston Brother's. That's the best not-so-expensive pizza around. If you like truffles at all, you should get them shaved on top. Will change your life." That was probably more than Tuesday wanted to spend and when I mentioned the truffles, she made a face.

"Truffles? Isn't that chocolate?"

"Are you serious?" She nodded.

"Someday, you will eat something covered in truffles and you will fall in love, Tuesday," I said with complete confidence.

"Yeah, I'll stick to my meat lover's thanks." Now I was the one making a face.

"Can we get a half-and-half?" If I was being honest, I could pack away almost an entire pizza by myself, but I didn't want to be too greedy since she was paying.

"How about we just get two pizzas? They have a special. We can get wings and drinks too. Do you eat wings?" Hell yes I ate wings, but I also appreciated that she asked.

"Sounds great." Now I wouldn't have to worry, and I'd get my own pizza. I texted Zee and said I was set for dinner and they texted me back asking for details and I said I'd fill them in when I got back. I wouldn't think about that right now. I wasn't going to think about anything but food, and maybe Tuesday's arms.

Tuesday put in her order and then handed me the phone to pick. I selected the spinach and artichoke pizza with feta and olives. I was feeling Greek tonight. Tuesday had added honey barbecue wings, which was perfect for me. I selected a drink and added it to the order.

"Thanks for this," I said, handing the phone back so she could put in the order. Once she did, I wasn't sure what to do next.

"You want to watch something?" She went over and grabbed a remote and walked over to where there was a TV bolted into the wall that I hadn't seen before.

"Uh, sure," I said. Tuesday pulled down two of the wooden boxes and set them up.

"Sorry I don't have anything fancier. I have some towels if you want something softer. I'm getting some benches too, but they haven't come in." The place was really coming together. So many changes in a short period. It looked like a gym now and not an empty prison-like space. Still not my aesthetic, but I was sure the kinds of people who liked CrossFit would enjoy the space.

Tuesday found a remote in the metal desk and brought it

over before getting some fresh towels from a converted bookcase right next to it. She handed me a few and I spread them out on the box to make it a little more comfortable.

Tuesday flipped on the television and started scrolling through the options on a popular streaming service. This was yet another time when I realized that I knew absolutely nothing about her but that she was my landlord, she liked CrossFit, she had two turtles, and she enjoyed pissing me off. As far as what she liked to watch, I had no clue.

"Have you seen this one?" she asked, bringing up a documentary about a grisly murder.

"Uh, no? Is that what you want to watch?" I wasn't a fan of anything about crimes. It just freaked me the hell out that something would happen to me. I didn't know how people could watch that stuff. Zee loved it, but I always hid when they had that stuff on.

"Just checking," she said, and then went to a classic show that I wasn't a fan of.

"How about this?" she asked, and I shook my head. It took five more tries before she landed on something I would consider watching. Guess we didn't have much in common in the show-watching department either.

I agreed to watch a documentary about the early days of strength training. I loved me a good documentary, as long as it wasn't about murders or kidnapping or people committing mass suicide. No thank you. Give me documentaries about the brain, or food, or capitalism and I was all over it.

Tuesday was quiet and sat on her own box, in spite of there being enough space for both of us to fit on mine. I tried not to read too much into that.

My stomach made a sound loud enough for us both to hear it.

"Do you need something now? I have some protein bars,"

she said, pulling out a box from behind the desk. "I have peanut butter, chocolate, and vanilla." She held them each up. They looked like the kind of protein bars that tasted like pure sawdust, but I was desperate. I could go upstairs and grab something, but these were right here.

"Peanut butter," I said, holding my hand out. She tossed it to me and I caught it. I read the ingredients first, and it seemed okay. I tore the wrapper off and took a bite. It wasn't as bad as I thought it was going to be, which was nice.

"Water?" Tuesday asked, and then tossed me a fresh bottle.

We settled in and I pretended I was watching the documentary, but I was watching Tuesday. I didn't think she could tell, but then she said, "if you'd rather stare at me than the TV, I can turn it off." My face flamed red and I looked at the screen.

"Sorry," I mumbled, even though that was admitting that I'd been looking at her.

"It's okay, you can admire me." If there was one thing she didn't lack, it was self-confidence. Somehow, that put her attractiveness level through the roof. It had already been hovering around the ceiling anyway.

I sighed and she gave me a fraction of that smirk that I'd seen last night. I wanted to slide off the box and onto the floor.

The pizza arrived a short while later and I attacked my box as soon as Tuesday put it next to me on the box.

"Do you want wings?" she asked, as I shoved one third of the first piece in my mouth.

"Yes please," I said around the mouthful. She must have understood because she tossed a few wings in the pizza box.

"I thought that I was going to eat you under the table, but I may have underestimated you." I finished my first slice and without even pausing, I went for the second. I was going to have to pace myself so I didn't eat this entire thing plus wings. That path only led to regrets.

I didn't have time to talk to her until I had finished my fourth slice.

"That's better," I said, patting my stomach and then going for the wings.

"I thought you were going to be vegan or something," Tuesday said.

"Nope. I've done periods of being vegan, but I feel like it's not a good diet for me to get everything I need, so I didn't follow it for long. I'm guessing you're not vegan either?" There were at least four kinds of meat on Tuesday's pizza. Maybe more than that.

"Not for me," she said, sucking sauce from the wings off her fingers. The action made certain areas of my body heat and tighten and tingle. I wasn't going to think about Tuesday licking things other than her fingers. That would be a very, very bad idea. Those thoughts were best not thought, or saved for nighttime when I was in bed alone.

I ate all my wings and then went for two more pieces of pizza before I decided to stop. That was one more piece than Tuesday and I grinned at her.

"Ha, I win."

"You have sauce on your chin," she said, motioning. I wiped my chin with my napkin and it came away covered in sauce. Guess I'd made a mess of myself. "And it's on your shirt."

"So it is," I said, looking down. I was usually a mess when I ate, and I'd been an extra mess because I was so hungry. I hadn't cared even a little bit what I'd looked like. Probably should have.

Tuesday tossed the boxes and came back to sit on the box. What now?

"I should get home." We hadn't really talked, and the evening felt unfinished.

"Color me officially impressed with your pizza consumption. I will not underestimate your appetite again."

"Thank you," I said. "I'm pleased to have impressed you." Tuesday pulled her feet up on the box and sat cross-legged facing me.

"You're gonna leave now." It wasn't a question.

"I mean, yes? I need to go home. The kitties need me."

"Don't you have a roommate?"

"Yes, but I miss them. Don't you miss Percy and Mary?" The tension in her face lessened at the mention of the turtles.

"Fine, I get it. Plus, I'm kind of an asshole." She got off the box and picked it up, carrying it back over to stack it with the others.

"I don't know what you want from me," I said, and she gripped the edge of the box and spoke without turning around.

"I don't know either," she said, her voice low.

The air in the large room changed so fast that I couldn't keep up. Tuesday turned around and the look she gave me was so intense, it was a wonder she didn't singe my clothes.

"I don't know what I want from you, Sutton." The pizza felt like cement in my stomach. Flutters broke out on my skin and I didn't know what to do, except that the next few moments were pivotal. Everything was about to change.

"You should go," Tuesday said. "You should really go."

"I can't," I said, telling the truth. "Whenever I come down here, I can't seem to make myself leave." Why was I telling her all this? I didn't want her to know any of this.

"It can't be my sparkling personality," she said, taking one step toward me. I inhaled slowly.

"I don't know what it is." More truth.

"What do *you* want from *me*?" she asked.

"I don't know." We were both at a loss. Tuesday took

another step, and then another. Blood raced through my veins, my heart pumping in double time.

Tuesday was less than four feet in front of me now. It would be wonderful and terrible if she came closer. I couldn't decide which was worse.

My lower lip trembled, as if in anticipation of something. Calm down, lips. You're not getting kissed. At least, I didn't think so. Of all the absurd notions, Tuesday kissing me. I still probably had pizza all over my mouth. I wasn't looking my best, that was for sure. Not my most kissable moment.

"Do you want me to step closer, Sutton?" I melted at the sound of my name. Now I was full on shaking and I needed to do *something*. I couldn't handle the suspense anymore.

"I don't know. What will happen if you do?" Wasn't that the question? Anything could happen. Unicorns could bust through the wall and stampede us to death. The ceiling could collapse. Someone else could walk in. Tuesday could kiss me. It was all up in the air.

"Mmm, I'm not sure either, and I don't know if I want to find out. You completely perplex me, Sutton Kay. In every possible way." Her voice was low and as thick as the tension between us. It had always been there, since that first day, but this time it was palpable. I could taste it.

"I can't figure you out," I said. "I don't know if I want to."

"That's probably wise. I'm not sure I'm worth figuring out." A shadow passed behind her eyes, like a cloud. There were deep layers to Tuesday, and I'd have to dive a long way to get to them all, if I even could. And I didn't know what would happen to me if I tried. I didn't want to drown.

"Oh, you definitely are. I'm not sure if I'm the right person to do that, though."

My phone vibrated and scared the shit out of both of us. The moment snapped, as if it had been sliced by a knife. I could finally make my feet move and go get my phone. It was Zee asking for an update on when I'd be home. I knew they were just being nosy because they cared, but still. I was frustrated and grateful for the interruption. What might have happened without it?

"Someone checking up on you?" Tuesday asked as I typed out a response to Zee.

"Just my roommate. They're a little protective." Tuesday crossed her arms.

"Do they think you need to be protected from me?" Tuesday slipped into using Zee's pronoun without a hitch. Yet another finger pointing to Tuesday being potentially queer. Plus, there was the sexual tension that was so intense that no one could have mistaken it for anything else. Fed up, I decided some bluntness was in order.

"Only if you're trying to seduce me. Are you trying to seduce me, Tuesday?" I couldn't believe the words that came out of my mouth. Who had I become in her presence? I should just flounce out of the room right now on that note and leave her gaping behind me, astonished by my sexy boldness.

"Wow, come right out and ask why don't you? Have I given any indication that that's what my goal is?" she asked, and I faltered.

"Am I the kind of person you might seduce?" What a completely ridiculous conversation.

"Are you asking if I'm attracted to you?"

"Well, *me*, but also women in general?"

Tuesday hid a grin and looked down at the floor.

"Is that what you're getting at? Wondering if I fly the rainbow flag?" I'd never heard anyone put it that way.

"I mean, yes. You don't have to tell me. It was rude to ask." Probably, but I still really wanted to know.

"Do you think I'm attracted to you?" Now I was starting to

get pissed off again. She was turning this around on me and I didn't like it.

"I asked you first," I said, which was the most childish response I could come up with.

Tuesday rolled her eyes.

"Fine, I'm going home. Thank you for the pizza and wings." This time she let me leave and, although my stomach was full, I was left unsatisfied.

Chapter Seven

"Tell. Me. Everything," Zee said, putting their hands on my shoulders and pushing me down on the couch before sitting next to me, their chin in their hands.

"Do I have to?" I said, but we both knew the answer to that. Yes, I did.

So I told Zee mostly everything, leaving out the chaos that had been happening in my body, and my random mental commentary. They didn't need to know every little detail.

"So you still don't know if she's queer?" I shook my head and Cappy clawed her way up my leg and into my lap. Her little claws were like needles, but she was so cute about it that I just let her do it and grinned through the pain.

"Nope. But reading between all of the lines, I'm guessing yes. If she wasn't, I feel like she wouldn't be teasing me and fucking with me like this, right?" Zee sighed.

"You won't know until she tells you." I'd tried to get her to tell me and it hadn't worked out and I'd gotten annoyed and left, so I was going to wait before I tried again.

"Plus, do you *want* her to be queer and potentially into you?"

"No," I said too quickly. Zee smiled at me and picked up Mocha.

"You're totally into her. I know you don't want to be, but you can be into someone without liking them. I do it all the time." It was true. Zee had a wild period where they were having fling after fling and I would see a different guy every week. I'd gotten a little concerned and asked them about it, but they said that they were just having fun and were using protection, so what was the harm? Once they put it that way, I knew they were right. I'd always been more of a relationship person, even though my relationships hadn't ever gotten super serious. I'd never given everything to someone I'd been with. I wasn't sure if I knew how. Doing that seemed too dangerous. Let myself be completely open and vulnerable to getting my tender heart smashed into a million pieces? No thanks. We'd always broken up before things had gotten that far.

"You look like you're thinking really hard over there," Zee said.

"Just pondering my past failed relationships. As one does." Zee made a face.

"You don't need to be doing that. And you don't even know if she wants to be with you, so don't get all worked up about it yet. Figure out if she's even available, and if she's into you, and then go from there. Don't put the sex before the horse." I snorted.

"Don't put the what before the what?" I couldn't believe they'd just said that.

"They used to say not to put the cart before the horse, but that's ridiculous because we don't use horses anymore, so I changed it to be modern." They said it as if they'd made complete and total sense.

"That's not how sayings work, Zee." They huffed.

"Well, that's how they should work. Language changes all

the time, so why can't I change it?" So that was a good point, but the other saying probably wasn't going to take off.

"But you knew what I meant," they said.

"I guess?" That sidetracked us into talking about various sayings that didn't work for modern times, but that people still used. I was glad for the topic change.

"Don't think that this means I'm not going to stop asking about Tuesday, because I don't have a lot of interesting things going on in my life and until I find my next boyfriend, you're my source of entertainment." I glared, but it was the least I could do for them. If I wrote out a list of all the shit Zee had done for me, it would be a mile long. I couldn't slack in the friendship department because they were so fucking good at it. The least I could hope for was being half as good.

I made jazz hands and pretended to dance.

"Yeah, that's more like it. Dance, Sutton, dance!" They clapped and I got up and did a little booty shake. That turned into a full-blown dance party, complete with picking up the kittens and trying to get them to dance with their little paws.

"I don't think they get what's going on," I said to Zee after a little while. We put the kitties down, but then they begged to be picked up again, so we danced a little more gently and they seemed to like that.

"Great, now they're going to beg for slow dances every night now." Zee swayed with Mocha, who had her eyes closed and her head on Zee's shoulder. It was such a precious moment I wanted to pick up my phone and take a picture, but I didn't want to put Cappy down, who was pawing at my shirt and begging for head rubs.

"Needy little beggar," I said to her. "Every day should end with kitty dance parties."

Zee made kissy faces to Mocha who was still asleep.

The dance party made me think about Tuesday's turtles

with their little hats. I wondered if she took them out of their tank and had dance parties with them. Granted, it would be impossible to tell if the turtles were having a good time. They weren't exactly known for their expressiveness. Something told me that a person who put hats on their turtles wouldn't turn down a turtle dance party. Maybe even a turtle rave with a DJ and strobe lights. The thought of that made me burst out laughing.

"What's so funny?" Zee asked.

"Nothing," I said, still giggling to myself. "Nothing at all."

～

I DIDN'T cross paths with Tuesday for an entire week. Either I missed seeing her, or she was hiding from me. Her car was in the parking lot, but whenever I went past the gym and glanced in, she wasn't in there. There were no more packages in front of my door, or music that was up too loud. She also didn't come to yoga.

My week was busy, but quiet, and it was strange how much had changed since Tuesday had bought the building. No longer did the smells of coffee and soft chatter from the shop below waft up into the studio. I wondered what it would be like when the gym opened. I'd even had a thought that we could do a promotion together to offer discounted classes at both our places. No idea if she'd go for that or not.

The week after that, I walked into the studio to find strange people replacing the ceiling tiles, installing security cameras, and doing a myriad of other things. I asked at least three guys who was in charge before I was directed to "Bruce" who seemed to be the one directing traffic. He was busy on his phone, but finally gave me the time of day.

"Can I ask you what the hell you're doing?" Maybe I

should have been a little nicer, but seriously, what was happening? I hadn't authorized any of this.

"I'm the new building manager. I got a work order and I showed up. You can take it up with your landlord." Bruce was brusque and went to answer a question from one of his guys.

"I have a class coming in in an hour. Are you going to be done by then?" I could only hope.

"Nope. We'll be done around five, and then we'll be back tomorrow until five." This was a nightmare.

"I have classes," I said, and Bruce just shrugged.

"Take it up with the landlord," he repeated.

"Oh, I will," I said, and stormed downstairs to the gym after a few seconds of getting over my shock.

I slammed the door open to find Tuesday working out in shorts and a sports bra. I only let my attraction register for a second before I started yelling.

"You cannot be fucking serious, Tuesday. You hired people to come and work on the studio without even telling me and now I'm going to have to cancel all my classes for two days and what the fuck?!" I threw my hands up in the air and she put the barbell down.

"I left you a note," she said, in an irritatingly calm voice. "They could only get me in today and tomorrow and I had to take it."

"You left me a note," I said. "You couldn't have called or texted?"

Tuesday just blinked at me. I knew she had my number.

"Fuck, Tuesday. This is a huge problem for me." I was already starting to panic with all the people who were going to be pissed off about missing their yoga. I was going to have to offer refunds and deal with that and hope that people would come back and not hate me forever.

"Whoa, calm down. It'll be fine. You just offer free classes.

People will be fine. Shit happens all the time. Hell, have the classes down here." She put her hand on my shoulder and I shook it off. I didn't want her to try and comfort me. It was patronizing when she'd caused this situation in the first place. I also didn't like her seeing me be this unraveled and vulnerable.

"Listen, we can move shit around down here and you can have your classes. We've got the sound system and showers and everything." I wanted to shove her away and tell her to go fuck herself for putting me in this position, but it really was the only viable solution, other than cancelling classes.

Now I was going to have to send a lot of emails and texts and post on social so people knew what was going on.

"Do you have a computer?" She did, and I was able to log-on to my check-in system from the gym, while Tuesday moved shit around and then brought all the mats, blocks, bolsters, chairs, and towels downstairs.

"I've also got water and so forth," she said, pointing to two coolers. "Water and drinks are on me. For your trouble."

"Thanks," I said in a sarcastic tone.

"Look, I'm sorry about this. But it had to be done." That was the first time she apologized, and it was overdue. Someone needed to teach her how to better interact with others and it wasn't going to be me.

I typed up a few signs and got them up on the studio, plugged my phone in with the studio music and set about trying to figure out how many mat spaces I could get in here. Luckily, the space was big and open, so I would have about as much room as both studio rooms combined. Everyone was just going to get real cozy in one room instead of two.

I started posting and sending emails and my first confused students arrived about a half hour later. They looked at the gym with skepticism and a little bit of horror. It would have been funny if I wasn't so worried about people being mad at me for the interruption in our regular service. We'd had building issues before, but I'd always dealt with them and people had been understanding. Pipes burst, roofs leaked, heating broke, etc., but there was something about this that really made me worry.

Priya came early to take class and didn't seem thrilled with the whole situation, but I told her that we were going to have to make do with what we had and she unrolled her mat and didn't complain after that.

A few people were visibly annoyed that we were down here, but once I got them on their mats and started class, they seemed to chill out. Tuesday made herself scarce during the classes and went back to the tiny little office way in the back of the gym and shut the door. I was grateful for that. I didn't need her watching me try to contain all this chaos.

The noise from upstairs was constantly distracting, but I got through my first class and then took Priya's. It was nice to be on the mat, even if I had to keep making sure I didn't smash myself into a rack of barbells.

I taught another class and then I had a little bit of a break. Tuesday poked her head out of the office.

"Can I come out now?" she asked, and I rolled my eyes.

"Yes, you didn't have to exile yourself. It's your gym."

"Yeah, well. I figured the least I could do was not be lurking around while you're doing your thing." She came out and went to the cooler to grab one of the fitness drinks I always saw in her hand.

"You going to take class? You might as well, if you're going to be here," I said, going for a water. I was going to run upstairs and get a kombucha later, but right now, I needed lunch.

"Maybe," she said. "Right now I need to eat something or else."

"Or else what?" I asked.

"You don't want to know." She'd put a shirt on, so I didn't have the image of her abs right in front of my face. "You want to get something?"

Every other time I'd eaten with her, I'd been mad at her by the end. Maybe this time would be different?

"Okay. But you have to promise not to piss me off more than you've already pissed me off today. I can't handle it." She laughed softly.

"I can't promise that, but I will do my best, how's that?"

I guess that was as good as it was going to get.

"Fine," I said and grabbed my bag. "Where to?"

∽

WE ENDED up at a chain burrito place by mutual agreement. All I wanted was nachos with extra cheese and guac. Tuesday got tacos and a burrito and rice, but I wouldn't expect anything less from what I'd seen her eat already.

"I really am sorry about the repairs. I've gone back and forth with that guy for months and this morning he let me know at six in the morning that these two days were the only ones that would work for months and I was so fed up and tired I just said yes. I didn't think about how it would affect you and I'm sorry about that." Wow. This was a Tuesday I hadn't encountered before.

"Thank you," I said, stunned. "I don't know what it's like to own a building. That sounds like a pain in the ass." She sighed and bit into her first taco.

"Tell me about it," she said, after she'd chewed and swallowed. She always ate so delicately, it was still a shock. It made me self-conscious about my own eating habits.

"How did you come to own the building?" I asked. I'd been

dying to know ever since she took over. She'd signed a waiver when she'd started at the studio and so I knew that she was only five years older than I was. Still pretty young to own real estate in the city.

"Do you really want to know?" she asked.

"I mean, yes? That's why I'm asking." I had all kinds of theories in my head. I wanted to know if any of them were right.

"I'm not sure that you do. It's not a rosy story. I didn't win the lottery or cash in a big investment." I hadn't thought so.

"Do you want me to guess?" I asked after a few more moments of silence.

"No, I'll just tell you. Now I'm making it into something it's not." Curiosity was going to be my end. My nachos were forgotten in the face of this tantalizing piece of information that made up the picture of Tuesday.

She put down her burrito and wiped her hands.

"Both my parents died. There. That's it. I got a bunch of money when they died since I'm an only child and I decided to invest in having my own gym. You were just a casualty of that decision."

"Oh, shit," I said before I could think about if that was the right thing to say or not. "I'm so sorry, Tuesday. Holy shit." I had never wanted to hug someone so much in my life.

She waved her hand, but her chin trembled for a moment before she picked up one of her tacos and started eating again.

"It's not a great story and it's a bit of a conversation killer, so I definitely don't lead with it when people ask about my life." I could see why. I wasn't sure what to say to her now.

"Do you want to talk about it, or do you want me to ask you to show me more pictures of the turtles?" I asked. I'd let her decide.

Tuesday gave me a long look with those eyes, and they were

less like ice now, more like lasers. Shooting into every nook and cranny to expose me.

"I'd rather talk about the turtles," she said, and her shoulders lowered, just a little bit. They'd been creeping up, as if talking about her parents made her stressed out. Why wouldn't it? Of course I was curious what happened, but if she didn't want to talk about that, I wasn't going to press because I wasn't a fucking monster.

"I had a dance party with Zee and the kittens. You should try that with the turtles. Do a turtle rave." Her face softened into an almost smile and then we discussed what kind of music one would play at a turtle rave at great length. That got us to talking about our favorite workout songs and Tuesday asked me about yoga music and I told her about the yoga rapper that I couldn't stand and then that led to talking about bad fitness music and before I knew it, I had to get back to the gym to teach another class.

"Thank you," I said, and she gave me a quizzical look. "For telling me about your parents. I know that can't have been easy. And if you ever want to talk about it, I'm here. And if you want to not talk about it, I'm also here for that." I thought about touching her on the arm, but that might be weird, so I didn't.

"That means a lot," she said, and we left the burrito place and walked back to the gym.

This was the first time I'd ended a meal with Tuesday not being angry with her, which had to be some sort of progress.

～

I MADE it through the rest of the day and through the next with my unorthodox classes and minimal complaining from my students. Tuesday stayed mostly in her office, but she came out on the last night after I'd cleaned up.

"I can carry those up," she said, pointing to the stacked mats.

"No, it's fine. I've got this," I said, but she just ignored me and picked up a bunch of them.

"Showoff," I muttered. Tuesday never let a chance slide by to show how strong she was. On one hand, it was irritating. On the other, she was hot as fuck and watching her ass as she walked up the stairs was one of the highlights of my week.

Between the two of us, we got everything upstairs and back to where it was supposed to be. The studio did look nicer and I had better security, so that was good as well. This was a fine neighborhood, but you never knew what could happen, and I wanted to make sure that everyone was safe.

Tuesday took me through everything and taught me how the security system worked. She'd had to update my existing system to match the one she'd installed downstairs that was top of the line. Even though it had been a horrible two days, I was glad it had happened. I'd never let Tuesday know that because then she'd be insufferable about it.

It was late and I wanted to go home, but once again, I didn't want to leave her.

"So, since we're opening in less than two weeks, are you going to sign up for your first class? I didn't forget about the dare." Of course she hadn't. I hadn't either. I wished I could call the whole thing off, but I wasn't going to do that. Tuesday might be more into dares, but I could get competitive when I wanted to. When I'd first started yoga, my main focus had been on getting as flexible as possible as quickly as possible. To no one's surprise but my own, I got injured and was told to slow the fuck down. It had taken a lot to come to terms with letting my body go at its own pace and being okay with that.

CrossFit was something else entirely. I still had no idea what it was, even though I'd watched some videos online. Everyone seemed SO fit and just completely ripped, like Tuesday. My body wasn't bad, but you couldn't count my abs, or see every single muscle group in sharp relief.

"It's not going to be bad," she said.

"I'm calling bullshit on that. I've seen some videos and there's nothing easy or gentle about what I've seen. I'm not ashamed to say that this whole thing is terrifying." I gestured upwards at the ropes and rings hanging from the ceiling. "It looks like torture."

Tuesday grabbed one of the ropes and started swinging it a little.

"Some people would say molding yourself into a pretzel is extreme. It's all about perspective. And you'll do an intro class first. We'll go over all the movements and how to do them and you'll be in it with other people who don't know what they're doing either. You already have a fit body, so it will just take some adjusting to learn the new movements. You'll be fine." I wish I had her confidence. I still didn't know if I wanted to do this, but I was going to give it a try. That was the best I could do.

"I'll give it a shot. One class."

Tuesday tried to hide a smile, but didn't think quickly enough.

"I'm really going to enjoy this," she said, letting go of the rope.

"Stop gloating. You have no idea, I could be amazing at whatever this is going to be." I hadn't really considered that, but maybe I would be good at it. Maybe I'd be the best.

"You do surprise me, Sutton. I'm not counting you out yet, but we'll see how you feel after a few rounds of burpees." I'd heard that term, but I had no idea what it was. I wasn't going to tell her that, so I just pressed my lips together and then looked at my phone. Late. It was very late and I was famished. For a moment, I considered asking her if she wanted to grab dinner as well, but I'd just had lunch with her yesterday, so I didn't know if that would be too much in one week.

So instead, I said goodnight and left with a pain in my chest, and a feeling of things between us being unfinished. As if we kept leaving with an ellipse at the end of our interactions and I never knew where we were going next. I didn't know where this was going with Tuesday, and I was afraid to find out, but there was a thrill with that fear. The thrill of flinging yourself into the complete unknown with no backup plan. The only other time I'd done anything like that was opening up my studio in the first place, and look how that had turned out.

When I got home, there was a direct message from Tuesday. It was a video of the turtles swimming around with music in the background. She'd moved the phone so it looked like a music video and I swear I could hear her making beatbox noises as well.

"What are you smiling about?" Zee said, looking over my shoulder.

"Nothing," I said, dropping my phone on the floor. The kittens jumped at the noise and ran away to hide under the couch.

Zee snatched my phone before I could get it, but then they handed it back to me.

"You don't have to show me. But I'm interested in whatever gave you that goofy smile." I didn't think I'd been smiling all that much, but I maybe I had been.

"It's nothing," I mumbled. I unlocked my phone and sent Tuesday back a smiling emoji. I would have to send her a picture of the kittens later. This seemed like a non-threatening way to talk back and forth with her. No pressure, just cute animals.

"Okay, okay," Zee said, putting their hands up. "I'll just live in suspense. How was work? Did you get through having to deal with your landlord all day?" I said that it had been fine and left it at that.

"Just fine? You've used a lot of words about Tuesday and none of them have been 'fine,' unless you're like 'she's so fine.'" I made a face.

"I would never say that about someone." Not even Tuesday. Okay, maybe Tuesday.

"Have there been any new developments?" Zee asked.

"Uh, no? Not really." There hadn't been, today. I'd told them about the lunch from yesterday, but I didn't talk about Tuesday's parents. That seemed too personal to tell anyone else about. She'd told me that in confidence and even though she hadn't asked me to not tell anyone else, I could get the feeling that she didn't want me sharing it like a juicy piece of gossip.

"Okay, okay, I'll stop badgering you. Come on, I'm making grilled cheese and tomato soup." I followed them into the kitchen and watched as they took a simple meal and made it totally elegant. Less than an hour later I was shoving bites of a grilled cheese sandwich on sourdough with smoked gouda and several other cheeses that had been dipped into a fresh tomato bisque.

"I don't know what I'm going to do if we ever don't live together because I'm going to starve." My parents, who had owned a restaurant, had always cooked and tried to teach me, but I always got distracted and burned things, or forgot ingredients, or didn't follow the recipe. I could microwave something, but as far as making dinners like Zee, I wasn't even close.

"You'll be fine. You can hire me as your personal chef. I'll cook for you every week and then drop it off." That didn't seem like a bad arrangement.

"Won't your husband object?"

Zee shook their head and sipped their soup.

"He'd better not or else he won't be my husband. Any man who can't handle my friendship with you is a man I don't need in my life." I raised my spoon and they clinked it with theirs.

"Amen to that. Same goes for me and a wife, if I can ever find one. It's not looking so great right now." I'd never even gotten close to that kind of commitment. I'd never even lived with a girlfriend.

"Oh, you'll be fine. I think the time is nigh for you finding someone. I just have a feeling." Mocha jumped up and tried to paw at my spoon, but I moved it so that she couldn't get it.

"You wouldn't like this, trust me." I held up my phone and took a video of Mocha sniffing the soup and then recoiling. It was so fucking cute. I sent it immediately to Tuesday without thinking.

Zee and I finished our dinner and watched a few episodes of our favorite show before I took the kitties and got in bed with a book. I had another message from Tuesday, this time she was trying to get the turtles to do tricks and failing miserably. I got a little glimpse of where she lived and what I saw looked nice. I still knew so little about her, so I scrolled through her social media again. She didn't have a ton of posts, and there were huge gaps where she hadn't put up anything for months. There were a lot of lifting pictures and videos and of course I watched all those. The weights were all in kilograms and I didn't feel like doing the math to convert them to pounds, but I could guess that it was a lot of weight.

My book forgotten, I lost myself in Tuesday's social pages for a few hours and before I knew it, my eyes were gritty and I was falling asleep on my phone. Oops? Finally, I plugged in my phone and set it on my nightstand so I couldn't keep scrolling.

This fascination with Tuesday was starting to impact my life, and I didn't know what to do about it. I wasn't just fascinated by her looks (although her body was fascinating), but I wanted to know more about her. I wanted to know how she'd felt growing up as an only child. I wanted to know if her heart had been broken, and how many times. I really, *really* wanted to know if she liked girls. We hadn't broached that topic again. I wondered if she thought I'd forgotten about it. I hadn't. It hung in the back of my mind whenever I was with her. I couldn't put my finger on why it mattered so much.

I was attracted to Tuesday, sure. But you needed more than lust to make a relationship. And I didn't want to date her. Hell no. Not even a little bit. Never, ever.

Not even if she begged me.

Chapter Eight

It was a relief to get back to normal and get back into my studio. Tuesday kept sending me turtle pictures and other random shit she thought would make me laugh. I found myself checking my phone a lot more often than I usually would, and Zee wouldn't stop commenting on it.

"I feel like you don't love me anymore," they said, rolling on the floor in front of me on Friday night. The two of us had gone out for sushi, but had come home and ordered dessert in. We were just waiting for our cake to get here. Living in a city was amazing like that. You could order just about anything at just about any time. It was a good thing I was so broke, or else I would spend all my money ordering various items to my house.

"Shut up, you're being dramatic," I said, sticking my foot in their face.

"Ew, gross!" They rolled away, swatting at my foot.

"I'm just . . ." I trailed off because I had no idea what I was doing with Tuesday. Were we friends? Just two people who sort of worked near each other? I didn't think that was the definition. I didn't think she would call me a friend if someone asked her if I was. I didn't know what she was to me. Too complicated. Far too complicated.

"You're just what?" Zee asked, getting up and then leaning back on the couch, avoiding both sleeping kittens.

"I don't know," I said. "I don't know what's going on with Tuesday and I don't know if I want it to keep going." Zee gave me a look. "What?"

"You definitely want it to keep going. It's written on your face. You have a thing for her." I sighed.

"That doesn't mean anything. I can like the way she looks and think her turtles are funny without it being some big thing." Zee smiled to themselves and shook their head.

"*What?*" I asked again. I was getting a little fed up with everyone reading too much into this.

"Sorry, sorry. I'm being annoying. I'll stop." They pulled my feet into their lap and started rubbing them. I closed my eyes and instantly my irritation melted away.

"That's not fair. I can't be cross with you when you rub my feet." I cracked one eye open to find Zee grinning.

"I know. It's something I've known for a long time and employ whenever I need to." I wanted to argue, but I shut my eyes and decided to just enjoy this.

My phone buzzed and I thought it was probably a message from Tuesday, but I didn't grab for it immediately, even though my fingers itched to reach for my phone. I waited for a least a minute, or so I thought.

"Wow, waiting thirty whole seconds. Impressive restraint," Zee said when I finally went for the phone.

"Shut up," I said, seeing another pic from Tuesday. This one was about working out. She'd started sending me goofy things about fitness and I loved them. Of course I had my group chat, but Tuesday understood certain things about my life in a way that some of my friends didn't. It was just . . .

different. I also didn't think about my friend's butts as much as I thought about Tuesday's. Not even remotely close.

I didn't think about anyone's butt as much as Tuesday's, and that included my own.

"I'm just teasing you. When I get my next boyfriend you can totally do the same thing. Not that Tuesday is your girlfriend or romantic partner." The last part was added hastily.

"That's right. She's not."

Zee started humming a tune I didn't know and went back to rubbing my feet, which distracted me from thinking about Tuesday again, but not for long.

∼

ANOTHER WEEK PASSED and before I knew it, Tuesday's gym was opening. I went downstairs the night before to see how she was doing, but I walked in to find her talking to someone who was almost as buff as she was.

"Oh, I'm sorry. I didn't mean to interrupt." I was so used to only seeing her in this space, it was strange to see someone else.

Tuesday's eyes flicked from me to the other person and back.

"It's okay," she said. "We were almost done." I wondered if she would introduce me to the other person, but she didn't seem like she was going to. So I did it.

"Hi, I'm Sutton. I own the yoga studio upstairs." I put my hand out to shake hers and hoped it wouldn't crush my fingers. She looked at my hand and then at me and then at Tuesday. Had she never been introduced to another human before? I wasn't doing anything out of the ordinary. People introduced themselves all the time.

"I'm Kiera, nice to meet you, *Sutton*," she said, and I

wondered why she was putting so much emphasis on my name. Then she looked at Tuesday, who was studying the floor. Had I missed something?

"I'm just going to go. I, uh, wanted to see how things were going for tomorrow." I'd come down to wish her luck, but I didn't know what the situation was with this Kiera.

"Kiera is one of my coaches," Tuesday blurted out. "She's just here working on some details for tomorrow. That's it." I looked at Kiera, who had a smirk on her face. She crossed her arms and her biceps bulged. Being around this much buffness was going to give me a complex.

"Great," I said, and wondered how to extricate myself from the room without it being weird. Or weirder than it was already.

"Well, I'm out. Nice to meet you Sutton, I'll see you tomorrow, Tues." Kiera grabbed a bag and slung it over her shoulder and was out of the room before I could say anything else. The door shut and I was left staring at Tuesday.

"I'm gonna head out too. Just wanted to wish you good luck and say that I'll be in class in a couple of days. If you need anything, I'll be in the studio all day. It's the least I can do after you let me use your gym space for two whole days." I had been wondering how I was going to do that. It wasn't a small thing she had done for me and I wanted to repay her for that kindness.

"I do," she said, raising her eyes and revealing that her face was entirely red, and I didn't think it was red from an intense workout.

"You do what?" I asked, and my heart started racing. I didn't know what she was going to say, but I knew it was going to change everything.

"I do like girls. Just so you know." I almost choked on my tongue.

"You do," I said after a few seconds of shock.

"I do." Our eyes locked and something unsaid passed between us. She took a shaky breath and then wiped her hands on her shorts, which drew my attention to her thighs, which were on full display.

"So do I. In case you didn't know that already. I like girls too." She nodded and picked at some calluses on her hands.

"That is good information to know."

"Is it?" I asked, my voice squeaking. My feet couldn't have moved if they tried. Tuesday looked up again and took a step closer.

"It is," she said, and reached her hand out. It hung in the air between us and I didn't know what she was going to do with it. She'd just admitted she liked girls, but did that include me? I still wasn't sure how I felt about her. Everything was so jumbled and confusing around her. I'd never been this conflicted in my life about another person.

After a moment, Tuesday dropped her hand and let out a soft chuckle.

"It's late. You should go."

"I should," I agreed, but I didn't move.

When I didn't, she made a sound of frustration. "Seriously, you should go."

"Why? What will happen if I don't?" I started to tremble with anticipation of what would come next. Tuesday and I were teetering on the edge of changing everything one way or another.

"You don't want to know."

The air was so hard to breathe, but I did my best.

"Maybe I do," I said, surprising myself. I wasn't bold. I wasn't a risk-taker (except for opening the studio, but that was a completely different thing than this).

"Are you sure?"

I nodded once.

Tuesday came so close that I could see that little brown fleck in one of her eyes and see how long her eyelashes were.

"What am I doing?" Tuesday said softly to herself.

"I don't know, but could you do whatever it is before I die from anticipation?" The words were out of my mouth before I could decide if they were the right words to say at this exact moment.

Tuesday's mouth lifted on one side into a smirk.

"If you keep being so sassy, I might not kiss that mouth of yours."

It was in that moment that I realized that I wanted to kiss Tuesday Grímsdóttir more than I'd wanted anything else in my entire life.

"If you don't kiss me, I'll die," I said. My words were just flying out of my mouth with no filter. Being around her made my brain malfunction.

"That seems a little dramatic, princess," she said, raising her hand and touching my cheek with callused fingers. Who would have thought that rough touch could be so sexy?

Her mouth drew closer and I decided to be the one who kissed *her*. There was no rule stating that Tuesday had to kiss me first. I could make a move. So I did.

Her lips trembled as I pressed mine against hers. The first kiss was a test. A brief touch to figure out if we wanted to keep going with this. That simple kiss was full of so much potential that I couldn't let her go without more. Tuesday's lips were soft and full and cradled mine with a delicacy I didn't anticipate from her.

I pressed closer, needing more contact. She was just a few inches taller, but I only had to tip my mouth up a touch for everything to be lined up perfectly. Her hand was still on my face, and her other moved to gripped my shoulder. I expected

Tuesday to kiss like she lifted: hard and fast. What a surprise to find that her kisses were slow and tender and sweet. So sweet.

Her tongue reached for my bottom lip, caressing it with care before I opened my mouth and let her do the same to the inside of my mouth. Our tongues swirled around one another, doing a slow dance that set my blood on fire. Now the fingers gripping my shoulder dug in and I heard the desperation in her gasping breaths.

That moment the tone of her kisses changed, and I caught a glimpse of the other side of Tuesday. The side with the demanding lips and tongue who ravished my mouth with a thoroughness that I could only admire. Not that I hadn't been kissed before this, but never like *this*. There was nothing beyond this kiss, beyond Tuesday.

Strange whimpering noises emerged from my throat and I was powerless to stop them. Tuesday smiled, and gave me a series of little nipping kisses before pulling back. My eyes opened slowly and it was like waking up after a vivid dream. I wasn't sure what was reality anymore. Tuesday had rearranged everything.

"Well," she said, her tongue licking her lips as if she wanted to savor the taste of me.

"Well, what?" I said, my voice weak.

"Well that was a surprise." Our faces were still so close, and I wanted to be kissing her again and not talking. I didn't need to talk ever again if it would take up time that we could spend kissing each other.

"A good surprise?" If she hadn't enjoyed that kiss then I would eat all of my yoga mats.

"Mmm, you could say that." Tuesday stepped back and released me. I swayed on my feet a little.

"What happens now?" That was the ultimate question. We'd crossed a boundary and now we were on a completely uncharted path. I still didn't know if she liked me. I didn't know if I liked *her*. The only thing I did know was that if I never kissed her again, I would probably die.

"I don't know," she said with a sigh. "I didn't anticipate this. I thought if I kissed you, it might be bad, or that we wouldn't click, or that it would get you out of my system. But that is not what happened." Oh. So she had been thinking about kissing me. That was an interesting revelation.

"Am I in your system?" She was certainly in mine.

Tuesday laughed a little.

"You could say that. I'm not even going to tell you what I did to try and get your attention." What was she talking about? I couldn't think right now.

"So you thought kissing me would help you stop thinking about me?" Tuesday walked over to one of the wooden boxes and sat down heavily on it. I followed her and sat on the box as well. She pulled her feet up and faced me.

"I don't know what to do here, Sutton. I'm not used to being in this situation and I'm not even sure this is anything that would work out. I mean, I don't know if I like you." She put her hands on her knees.

"That makes two of us, because I'm not sure if I like you either," I snapped. Our eyes met and we both grinned at each other.

"This is really weird," she said.

"Agreed."

"Weird enough not to want to kiss me again?" she asked, and leaned forward.

"No. I mean, yes. I mean, I want you to kiss me again. Definitely." My phone went off and I pulled it out of my pocket. It was Zee, asking if enchiladas were okay for dinner.

"My roommate," I said, typing that I did want enchiladas.

That sounded amazing right now. "Asking what I wanted for dinner."

"Your roommate, huh?" Tuesday asked, and I was confused for a second.

"They're literally just my roommate. They aren't into girls." Not even a little bit.

"Good to know." Tuesday got off the box and walked in a little circle. "So, I don't know what we're doing, and I don't know why we're doing it, but I think we owe it to ourselves to see what the hell this is. Don't you think?" I was up for that, and I told her so.

"I'll send you some turtle videos later," Tuesday said.

"That's not as good as kissing," I said, trying not to pout. I wasn't going to beg for more kisses, but also . . .

Tuesday laughed a little.

"Fair enough. But I'm not sure if we should kiss any more tonight." I felt the color drain from my face.

"Why not?" Oh crap, did she not want to kiss me anymore? Could I have blown it in the past few moments?

"Because if I kiss you again, I might not stop with kissing." She walked back to her little office and shut the light off. Looked like she was getting ready to lock up and go home. I also had kittens and enchiladas waiting for me and I was hungry and missed my babies. But *kissing*.

"And that's a problem because . . ." I trailed off and she groaned.

"You are stubborn when you want something, aren't you?" she said, grabbing her bag and then starting to turn off some of the other lights.

"Yes, you should probably know that about me now." I might not be an impulsive person, but I was stubborn as hell when there was something I wanted.

"Got it," she said, and shut all the lights off. The only illumination came from some of the windows and the glass front door where the light from the lobby came through.

"You're kicking me out," I said. "Rude."

"I'm not kicking you out. I'm ending the night because I don't want either of us to rush into anything that we might regret. I've done that before and I don't want to go down that road again." I saw her profile in the weak light and I could tell there was definitely more to it.

"There's so much I don't know about you, Tuesday," I said.

"Exactly. And I think there are some things you should know if this is . . . something. I still have no idea if that's what I want." Me neither. I started to walk toward the door and she followed me. I waited while she set the alarm for the gym, and then for the whole building. We walked out to our cars, which happened to be parked right next to each other.

"You're not a serial killer, are you?" I asked by way of goodbye.

"If I was, I wouldn't tell you, would I?" She winked and unlocked her door. "Goodnight, Sutton."

"Goodnight," I said, but she was already starting her car. She gave me a little wave before she pulled out. I sagged against my door and stayed there for a few moments. Holy shit.

"I KISSED HER," I announced, when I walked into the kitchen to find Zee taking the enchiladas out of the oven. Zee stared at me and stood up with the pan. Their oven mitts had FUCK and YOU written on them.

"You can't walk in and say something like that when I'm holding a hot pan. I almost dropped this, and then we wouldn't have dinner." They set it down on the stove and took off their oven mitts. "Now that our food is safe, you need to tell me every single detail."

They put their hands on my shoulders and pushed me toward the living room and onto the couch.

"The food can wait," they said. "I have to hear about the kissing. No, wait. Hold on." I was getting whiplash from this. I sat with the kitties and waited for Zee to come back. I was still in a state of shock about the fact that the kissing had happened at all. Part of my brain wasn't sure if it had.

Zee came back with two glasses of wine. The only bottle in the fridge had been one that I knew Zee had been saving.

"Really? You broke out the fancy wine for this?" I asked, taking the glass from their hand.

"Yes, now go." They pulled their feet up and put all their attention on me.

"I feel like I'm on the stage or something," I said. Zee waved their hand.

"Just get to the good stuff."

So, I told them (nearly) everything. When I heard the story out loud, it sounded unreal, even to me, and I'd just been through it.

They sat there and sipped their wine and were on the edge of their seat the whole time. My heart pounded a little bit in the retelling and my hands tingled.

"Well, well, well," Zee said, when I finished with leaning against my car in the parking lot.

"Did that actually happen?" I said, leaning back on the couch. Cappy climbed up onto my chest and licked my chin. "Now I'm getting kitty kisses. So many kisses for one day."

"I'm not going to lie, I'm a little jealous. I haven't had a good make out session in forever. I need to find someone to make out with. I'm going to sign up for that dating app again. If you know of anyone who would want to make out with me, send him my way." I said that I would.

"Maybe there will be someone at the new gym downstairs.

Would you go out with a CrossFit guy?" They pretended to think that over.

"Lots of muscles? Yeah, I think I could work with that." They grinned and rubbed their hands together.

"Okay, ew," I said, getting up. "Also, I'm starving. Can we eat now?" Zee dished out the enchiladas and I sipped my wine. This was a wine night. All I could think about was kissing Tuesday again. When would that happen? Tomorrow? I hoped so.

I couldn't get her out of my mind. My mind wouldn't stop replaying every single detail. Then my imagination picked up where reality had left off. What if we had gone further? What if she'd taken off her shorts and her sports bra? What if she'd removed my clothes? I opened my eyes and found both kitties staring at me.

"Okay, you need to learn about privacy," I said. I wanted to kick them out because it was creepy to be having sexy thoughts while being watched by two kittens. My lust had ignited, though, and I couldn't stop now if I wanted. Apologizing profusely, I picked them up and put them outside the door.

"Two minutes. Just give me two minutes." They stared up at me in betrayal. I spared a moment to feel like a horrible kitty mom and then closed the door and grabbed my vibrator from the drawer next to my bed. I was already so turned on that it really did only take about three minutes before I came, and came hard. I lay there for a second, but then the crying kittens jolted me back to reality. I got up slowly, since I was a little boneless from the orgasm. It had been a while since I'd had one that fast and that hard.

Floating a little, I went to let the kittens in. Both of them gave me glares of betrayal, but then hopped up on the bed and lay down.

"I'm sorry," I said as I put my vibrator away. "But you don't get it."

Only a few minutes later I was horny again and wanted to come, but I also couldn't banish the kittens a second time, so I just lay there and tried to think of un-horny things. It wasn't going very well. Every time I tried, my brain just went back to Tuesday. A naked Tuesday, lifting weights. Sweat-drenched and muscles popping. I didn't think I would be into that kind of person, but apparently, I was. Very into.

I couldn't get her out of my head and I wasn't sure if that was a good thing or a bad thing. A very bad thing.

Chapter Nine

THE PARKING LOT was packed the next morning with people coming to the gym opening. Tuesday had classes going all day, and balloons tied to the door handle and a big GRAND OPENING banner across the new sign for CrossFit 721. I still didn't know what the name meant, and I made a mental note to ask her about it.

I kicked myself for not getting her a little grand-opening gift, but I had plenty of time before my first class, so I walked down the street and got a gift card to the lunch place where we'd eaten together the first time, and then grabbed a card. They didn't have a "congrats on opening your CrossFit gym" card, but I picked one with a generic Congratulations! message and signed it with my name. I hoped she didn't read too much into the card. It was pretty innocuous, I thought.

When I got back, there was a class just getting out, so I had to wade through a bunch of sweaty people who had dazed looks in their eyes. I'd seen that look after a particularly intense yoga session. I finally made my way into the gym and found Tuesday moving boxes around and talking to Kiera and two other people. I thought about coming back later, but no doubt she was going to be surrounded by people all day. She happened to turn and met my eyes.

"Hey," I said, holding out the card. "I got you a little something. It's busy in here already. How are things going?" The other three people stepped back and Tuesday stepped forward to greet me. I wanted to kiss her, but I didn't know if I should. Probably not.

"Hey," she said, her voice rough and soft at the same time. "Thanks for coming by. It's been busy. I'm guessing that's because of the free classes, but I'm hoping we can convert some of the new people to regular memberships." I handed the card to her. "Thank you," she said, and I knew she meant it.

"You're welcome," I said, and waited for her to open it. Instead, she turned it over in her hands.

"I'm going to save it and open it later. It'll give me something to look forward to when I'm completely dead later from coaching. You should come by when you're done." She came closer and spoke in a low voice, so only I could hear her. "And you can kiss me, if you want. I don't think it's a good idea right now though." As much as I ached to kiss the crap out of her, I knew that she was right. If we kissed in front of all these people, we were going to have to give answers to questions we didn't even have the answers to ourselves.

"This is so weird," I admitted.

"I know. But I'm going to *think* about kissing you all day." I'd thought about kissing her all night so that was only fair.

"Come up for a kombucha on the house later, if you can," I said, and then waved to her before heading up the stairs to the studio. I cringed at the sound of the music bumping from below. CrossFit was loud. At least the way Tuesday did CrossFit. I guess I was going to have to get used to that.

I lit some incense and grabbed a green juice for myself. I needed it to get through today.

THE ENTIRE DAY WAS CHAOS. The door downstairs was constantly opening and closing, people were wandering up to the studio from downstairs, the music was loud and relentless, and there were constant bangs and clangs from the weights. I endured it all with a smile on my face and did my best to teach with the serenity my students had come to expect.

"That is *loud*," Ellen said, when she came to teach her class.

"Yeah, I know," I said, as she came over to take off her shoes.

"Is it going to be like this all the time? There are so many buff people downstairs, it's like an ad for steroids." I laughed and sat down next to her.

"Tell me about it. They keep coming up here and asking about yoga, but I can tell they think it's pointless and useless. I'm tempted to give them coupons or something to come and take a class, just to see them get their asses kicked." Ellen cackled.

"I would pay good money to see that. All those bros trying to keep their balance and failing. Timber!" That gave me a mental image of a bunch of CrossFit dudes in tree pose all falling one after the other and taking each other out. I couldn't help but smile.

"That would be worth selling tickets for." The phone rang so I had to get it and Ellen started getting ready for her class. I did a bunch of work while she taught and got a few little messages from Tuesday. This time it wasn't just funny pictures and turtle videos. There were cute flirty things now. Flutters broke out in my body, and it was hard to concentrate on work when I was thinking about her.

"You're in a good mood today," Ellen said, after she'd said goodbye to her last student. "Any new developments I should know about?" I didn't think I was going to be able to hide everything happening with Tuesday, but at least I could ask the people in my life to be nice and not ask me about it. Maybe.

"Oh, it's nothing. I don't know. I can't say." My cheeks were hot and I would have bet everything that they were red as hell.

"Interesting," Ellen said with a grin. "I am waiting on the edge of my seat here. Can you give me any details?" I shook my head. Any kind of details would point right downstairs and toward Tuesday.

"I'll tell you when I know what the hell I'm doing. If I ever do." Time would tell.

"Mmm, I can't wait. Let me know if you need someone to talk it out with. I'm always here." She patted my shoulder and then grabbed her bag.

"See you later," she said in a singsong voice.

"Bye," I said, drawing the word out. She chuckled as she got into the elevator. If there was anyone who could help me with questions of romance, it was Ellen.

Somehow I made it through the rest of the day and evening. I was absolutely starving by the time I was ready to leave, and I sent a message to Zee that I was going to order dinner and then pick it up on my way home. They wrote back with what they wanted and said they were glad that they didn't have to cook for once.

I glanced through the door into the gym and found that it was empty, except for Tuesday. She was on one of the boxes, eating something from a paper plate. Our eyes met and she smiled a little before getting up and walking over to let me in. She must have locked the door.

"How's it going?" I asked, and saw that she had cake on her plate. My mouth instantly started to water. I considered ripping the plate out of her hands, but that probably wouldn't end well for me or the cake.

"Good. Exhausted. Uh, you want some cake? You're looking at it like you want make out with it instead of me." I glanced up and realized I had been staring at the cake.

"I'm starving," I said as an explanation.

"Come on." Tuesday brought me to the back where there was a sheet cake on a bench. It had the logo of the gym on it, and was about 1/3 of the way eaten.

"You would think people would have eaten more, but no. They left me with all the sugar and processed flour." Tuesday shrugged and cut me a piece before stabbing it with a plastic fork and handing it me.

"I can help you with all of that," I said. "And so can my roommate. They'll eat anything, in large quantities." Zee could put away that whole damn cake in one sitting. Actually, if I didn't bring some home for them, they would probably murder me in my sleep.

"Please, take some. I definitely can't finish it all." I sat down and attacked the cake. It was just the right amount of pure sugar, and I almost moaned when it hit my tongue.

"Kiera and a few of my friends got me the cake. I told them not to, but they did it anyway." Tuesday poked at the cake and then set the plate down.

"That's nice of them. Was it a good day?" I shoveled more cake into my mouth. I was going to be high on sugar in a few minutes, but I seriously didn't care.

"Yeah, I think so." Tuesday sighed and sat back on the bench. "Time will tell. I had a few people sign up for memberships, so that's good. I just don't know if that energy will last, or if I'm going to make a go of this." I nodded, completely sympathizing.

"You'll always have that doubt. I'm almost two years in and

I still wonder if I'm ever going to feel like I've succeeded. My next goal is to open a second studio, but I'm nowhere near close to ready to do that." I'd need to get my membership up first, and definitely hire some more teachers, and maybe even a manager. I wasn't ready for that yet.

"You'll do it. In a few years you're going to have a yoga empire." I thought she was joking, but I couldn't really tell.

"I don't want to have an empire. Two or three studios would be enough for me. That might be more than enough, actually. I have no idea if I'd be able to manage multiple locations." I shuddered at the thought of all that work and the stress of paying rent on two places.

"So what you're telling me is the doubt and terror never goes away?" I scraped the last bit of frosting from the plate and eyed the cake. I could go for at least one more piece, if not two more.

"Yes, that's what I'm telling you," I said. "Sorry, I probably should have sugarcoated that better since you're just starting. But you're a franchise, so I'm guessing it's a little different, because you have corporate support behind you." I would never have that.

Tuesday shrugged. "Do you want some more cake?"

"Is it okay if I said yes?" She laughed and grabbed my late, serving me up another slab of the grocery store cake.

"It's always okay to say yes to cake," she said.

"Words to live by. You should put that on the wall. Right above your logo. CrossFit and cake. You'd have the only one in Boston." Tuesday stared at me as I devoured more cake. The sugar was just starting to hit me and I was going to be flying in a few minutes. I should probably cut myself off soon or else I was going to get drunk on cake.

"I'll add that to my business plan, but I don't think it would go over well with corporate." Probably not. I finished my second plate of cake and set everything aside.

"Now I'm ready for something sweeter," I said, licking the last of the frosting from my lips.

Tuesday looked puzzled for a second and then groaned.

"That was one of the worst lines I've ever heard."

I leaned closer to her and smiled.

"But is it working?"

She took a shaky breath.

"Maybe a little." I reached for her at the same time as she reached for me and we came together with a crash. It wasn't sweet and soft like we'd started last time. No, this was hard and a little bit vicious. Before I knew it, my back was on the floor and Tuesday's body was stretched out on top of mine. Her skin was hot and tight, and I could feel every single muscle. She was heavy, but I didn't care. She could press all the air out of my lungs and I wouldn't care at all.

Her teeth nipped at my lips and tongue and I bit her back. She seemed to like that, judging from the sounds she made. I could barely breathe and I think she noticed because she levered herself up with her arms.

Tuesday looked down at me. Her ponytail hung down on one side and brushed my arm, causing goosebumps.

"I'm blaming this on the cake," she said, her chest heaving. I was breathing pretty hard as well, and not just because she'd been crushing my lungs. Our hips were still pressed together and I couldn't concentrate on much but the fact that that was happening.

"Cake?" I said. There wasn't enough blood going to my brain. It was busy going to other areas.

"Mmm, maybe just a little bit on the cake," she said, brushing some of my hair out of my face. I kept it up when I taught, but I'd let it down earlier when I'd been in my office.

I couldn't fathom why we were talking about cake when we could be making out again.

"Come back," I whined, reaching to pull on the back of her neck to bring her mouth back to mine. She laughed softly.

"Demanding," she said, but it was as a term of endearment. At least I hoped so.

"Uh huh," I said before our lips met again. With one hand, she stroked the side of my face and then her fingers went to the side of my neck. She didn't know this yet, but neck kisses were a sure way to get me to completely lose my mind and probably take all my clothes off.

Tuesday stroked my neck while her mouth went back to work. She kissed with an intensity that let me know she wasn't thinking about anything else but this moment right now. It was almost overwhelming, and I still couldn't really breathe, but why did that matter?

Things ratcheted up a notch when her hips started to move. Then I was completely lost and I didn't have a coherent thought again. I couldn't think; I could only feel.

I wanted her. Bad. I wanted her to rip my clothes from my body and ravish me on this floor that was probably covered in a least fifty people's sweat. I didn't even care.

Of their own accord, my hands went to her hips, squeezing them and rocking my hips up to meet hers. Even through layers of clothing, the sensations were so intense that I didn't know if I could handle much more, and yet that was the word that came out of my mouth when she paused to change angles.

"More."

I expected her to come back to my mouth, but she kissed my nose as she gasped in a breath.

"I don't think that's a good idea, princess," she said, her voice hoarse.

"Why?" I guess I could only make one-syllable words.

"Because one of us has to be the sensible one. I guess it's going to be me." She removed her body from mine and I shivered at the loss of connection. I lay there, not knowing what to do.

"You going to be okay?" Tuesday stood over me, her hands on her knees as if she had been running and needed a break.

"I don't know," I said. Yay for three words!

"Yeah, me neither," she said, and put her hand out to help me get up. I reached for her and she helped me get to my feet, but then I wobbled so much that she had to put both hands on my shoulders to steady me.

"We should end this or else I'm going to fuck you on this floor and I don't think that's what you want," she said, and then my knees really did buckle.

I made an incoherent noise and she let go of me.

"Why are you so mean?" I finally said.

"Trust me, I'm suffering just as much as you are." She squeezed my shoulders and let go. I swayed on my feet. It wasn't fair that I was the only one who was so affected. Then I saw the pulse trembling in her neck and the fact that she was still having trouble breathing. That was a little better.

"I should go home?" I said, and it sounded like a question.

"Probably," she said, stepping closer to me as if she was going to kiss me again.

"What are we doing?" I said, asking the question that had been pounding in my head this whole time.

"I have no idea, but I think I want it to continue. I mean, not on the gym floor. We should probably take the kissing to another location next time." That made sense. "So, with that said, do you want to come over sometime?"

She was so cute about asking that it was an effort not to kiss her again.

"Can I meet the turtles?" That made her laugh.

"Yes, you can meet the turtles. Also, I'm beginning to think that you're more into the turtles than you're into me." I knew that I was into her, but I didn't know if I liked her yet, which was a strange situation to be in. I needed of find out if I liked her, or if this was all just pure lust.

"Well, I'm not going to make out with the turtles," I said.

Tuesday made a face.

"Ew, that is a disturbing mental image."

We both laughed and I managed to unstick my feet from the floor and start walking toward the door.

"Please take the cake from me," she said. "Seriously, if I have it in my house, I will consume the entire thing." If I had it in my house, Zee would eat the whole thing, but then I'd also have cake, so I agreed. She handed me the box and I balanced it with my stuff as she locked up and we went out to the parking lot.

"I'll see you tomorrow?" I said. "Do you maybe want some breakfast? I know it can be hard in the early days to remember to eat." I lived on bites of bars and green juice I chugged between classes and learning how the hell to manage a studio when I'd started. Zee used to take time out of their day to bring me food and force me to sit down and eat it.

"That would be . . . nice. Thank you." She seemed surprised at the gesture.

"Okay, so I'll message you tomorrow morning on my way in and you can tell me what you want." I could picture it now: I'd walk in with a bag of breakfast sandwiches and two coffee cups and she'd beam and kiss me.

"Okay," she said, and leaned on my car next to me. "I'm not really sure how to say goodnight to you anymore. A kiss seems appropriate, but I'm afraid if I kiss you now, I won't be able to stop." I didn't see the problem.

"So don't stop. We can just kiss here all night." Tuesday made a groaning sound.

"Don't tempt me. Let's just call it a night and I'll see you tomorrow morning. I'll send you more turtle videos later." She took my keys from me and unlocked my door, putting the cake in the passenger seat.

My phone buzzed with messages from Zee asking where I was and when I was going to be home for dinner. I got in the car and made it home somehow.

"You didn't answer me back, so I went ahead and made tacos, you're welcome," Zee called from the kitchen as I greeted the kitties. I wasn't completely sure how I'd gotten home, since I was still a little dopey from kissing Tuesday. I wondered if that would ever go away, or if it was just because everything with her was so new.

"I brought cake, you're welcome," I called to them. They popped out of the kitchen, a bag of lettuce in their hand.

"Did you say cake?" Their eyes lit up as if I'd brought home a bag of cash, or a really sexy man. Zee had cake lust, and so did I. It was one of the reasons we worked as roommates. A strong appreciation for cake, and for each other.

"Yup. Tuesday gave me the rest of hers, so you're allowed to have *some* of it. I want a little more." I wasn't going to tell them that I'd already had two pieces today. They didn't need to know.

"Okay, I approve of Tuesday," Zee said, grabbing the box of cake and cradling it like a baby.

"You haven't even met her," I said, as Zee made heart eyes at the cake.

"Doesn't matter. She gave you cake. Anyone who brings cake is fine in my book." I picked up the kitties and kissed their heads as they protested.

"So you're saying if Ted Bundy brought you cake, you'd get in his car?" Zee looked up at me in disgust.

"First of all, Ted Bundy is dead, and second, he never lured anyone with cake." The kittens squirmed to get down and I let them down so they could tumble around with each other.

"Can we stop talking about Ted Bundy?" I asked. Zee just carried the cake into the kitchen as if it was a precious item. They already had everything ready for the taco bar set out. I only made up three since I'd eaten so much cake. Zee filled their plate with half tacos and half cake.

"It's a balanced meal," they said.

"Hey, I'm not judging."

We sat down and Zee begged for a Tuesday update. I told them we'd kissed again and left out some of the more salacious details since I wanted to keep those for myself. Zee didn't need every little dirty detail.

"So, is this a thing now or . . .?" they asked, and I shrugged as I munched on my second taco.

"I have no idea. We haven't exactly gotten to the talking stage. It's like we're avoiding it because if we talk about it, then everything will change. Plus, this was only the first real day." My phone went off and it was a turtle video from Tuesday.

"You're smitten as hell, though. Just so you know," Zee said, moving from their tacos to the cake.

"I am?" I said. This was news to me.

"Yeah. You like her."

"I still don't know. I *want* her, but I'm still not sure about liking. I don't know a whole lot about her. She's not exactly an open book kind of person." Trying to read Tuesday was like trying to peel glued-together pages apart. She made you work for every little bit. It was work, and I wasn't sure if I was ready for that. Couldn't we just be make-out friends and have that be it? Then I didn't have to worry about getting my emotions all entangled, or risk my heart being broken.

Sooner or later, I was going to have to talk to her about what we were doing. I hoped it would be later. The idea of having that conversation made me feel like I was going to break out in hives.

"Do you want to come to spin this weekend with me?" Zee was a little more hardcore on the workout stuff than I was, and loved things like spinning and rock climbing and kayaking. I went with them sometimes, but it had been a while because I'd been so busy with the studio.

"Yeah, sure. I'm hoping that Tuesday will forget that I said I would do CrossFit."

"I'm guessing she won't, and she's waiting to spring it on you." That would be awful.

"Ugh," I said and picked up my last taco. "I don't wanna."

"You would if she told you to. I bet you would." I wanted to argue with them, but the truth was, if Tuesday begged me to do CrossFit, I would do it. I'd probably make them kiss me senseless afterward to make up for it, but I would do it. Now I had to hope that she wouldn't ask me.

Chapter Ten

She hadn't forgotten. It was the first thing she mentioned when I brought her a bag of breakfast sandwiches and a coffee the next morning. I wasn't surprised that she got a latte with three shots of espresso. If I drank that, it would probably kill me. I couldn't have that much caffeine in one sitting, but Tuesday sucked it down while making noises that turned me on so much I had to start thinking about non-sexy things.

"So, the gym has been open for an entire day and you haven't signed up for class. What's the deal?" She bit into her first sandwich and I froze as I raised mine to my mouth.

"Huh?" I said, but she didn't buy that.

"We have a Fundamentals class at seven tonight. I can have you sign a waiver and put you on the roster in about five minutes." I nibbled at my sandwich and tried to ignore the terror that had started to bloom in my stomach. Now that I was in the gym, and looking at all the equipment, I was nervous as hell.

"Maybe," I said and she finished her first sandwich and went for a second.

"No maybe. I dared you. I did yoga, Sutton. Me. Did yoga.

Twice. And I'm going to do it again. I stepped out of my comfort zone and it's time for you to do the same." I didn't like that she was calling me out and I also didn't like that she was right. When *was* the last time I stepped out of my comfort zone and did something that scared me? Not for a while. I couldn't put my finger on the last thing I'd done like that. My life needed a shakeup. I guess this was going to be it.

"Fine. I'll come. I have to teach, but I'll be done before seven. Is there anything I need to bring?" A slow swirl of anxiety started in my stomach, but I finished my sandwich and drank the rest of my coffee.

"You'll be fine," she said, patting my arm. "We're just going to go easy the first time. You'll learn how to do everything. You're already fit, so you're going to be miles ahead some of the other people." She got up and brought me a clipboard with a form on it. I filled it out and gave it back to her. Guess this was happening.

"Are you sure I won't die?" I asked, and she laughed.

"I haven't seen anyone die doing CrossFit yet, but you never know." I smacked her in the arm.

"Hey, I brought you breakfast. Be nice."

Tuesday tossed the clipboard on the ground and picked me up off my feet. I squealed and flailed a little and she set me back down but kept her hands on my waist.

"Is this nice?" she asked, and then kissed me. I couldn't answer her because my mouth was occupied, but I wasn't sure if it was nice. Kissing Tuesday wasn't merely *nice*. It was . . . everything. There weren't words that had been invented to describe what kissing Tuesday was like, at least not yet. Maybe I could invent some. Not right now since my brain wasn't working at full capacity.

Tuesday broke the kiss and smirked at me.

"Nice?"

"No," I said. "It's insulting to call that nice. It's beyond nice. Not even in the same galaxy as nice." She chuckled and tapped my nose with her finger.

"That's what I thought."

I wanted to kiss her some more, but we both had classes to teach and it might not be the best thing if her customers came in and found us sucking each other's faces off.

"I'll see you later tonight? Don't forget, Fundamentals at seven." My stress wasn't only for the newness of the class, but of doing something like that in front of Tuesday. I didn't want to look like a total loser in front of her. I guess it was only fair since I'd made her do yoga and had taken glee in her failing at certain poses. Fair was fair, but that didn't mean I had to like it.

"I haven't forgotten," I said, choking a little bit on air and coughing.

"You're going to be fine." She pushed me toward the door and I left, heading upstairs to my studio.

∼

I COULDN'T STOP WATCHING the clock the rest of the day. It was taunting me.

"You're so jumpy today," Priya said, when she came to teach the noontime class. "Is everything okay?"

"Yeah, just . . . I don't know. Just a little stressed." I wasn't going to tell her about Tuesday. I wasn't going to tell anyone but Zee about Tuesday.

"Anything I can do?" Priya was so lovely and I hated that I couldn't just tell her everything. Tuesday and I hadn't agreed that we wouldn't tell anyone about what we were doing, but it seemed implied.

"No, I'm just going to have some tea." Tea would certainly help take the stress about CrossFit away.

"Okay," Priya said, but she didn't sound convinced.

Ellen also asked me what was up, and even a few of my students asked if I was okay. Guess I couldn't hide my emotions as well as I thought I could. I assured everyone I was fine, that it was just a busy day at work and I would do some meditation and I was sure I'd be better tomorrow. If I was alive tomorrow. I didn't want to look up statistics on if anyone had died doing CrossFit and scare myself.

I knew I would need fuel to get through the workout, but eating dinner was a struggle. I'd grabbed a protein shake earlier and added that to my salad and avocado toast, hoping that would be enough.

I threw myself into doing paperwork and wished that there was some kind of emergency that would come up so I could cancel. I didn't want to do this.

No. I was going to do this. I had been dared and I was going to suck it up. I could only imagine the look on Tuesday's face if I told her I wasn't coming tonight.

"Let's do this," I said to myself, and did a quick ten-minute meditation to clear my head and cut down on some of my anxiety. It helped, and then I left my office, grabbed my stuff, and headed downstairs. The music was going and it was even louder down here. I didn't know how anyone could stand it.

I walked in to find a few people on the floor stretching and talking, and a few others looking around like they were lost and wanted to run away. I figured I probably looked like the latter.

Tuesday came out from the back and saw me. Her face lit up in a smile, but she quickly hid it away, as if she didn't want anyone to see her beaming at me.

I sat down on the floor and pretended to stretch like the other people. Tuesday walked by me, but she didn't give any indication that we knew each other. I was hoping she would come over and coddle me a little, but she didn't. She was treating me like everyone else. I probably should have talked to someone else in the class, but I was too nervous.

Instead I stared at the floor and tried to get my heart to stop beating so fast. After what seemed like an eternity, Tuesday turned down the music and started the class. I braced myself.

∼

AN HOUR later I knew how to do a squat, a press, a deadlift, and a bunch of other things I couldn't remember the names of. I did pull-ups, which weren't awful, and the push up position for CrossFit was the same as chaturanga, which was nice. At least that I knew how to do. Still, I collapsed on the floor at the end of the workout, chest heaving and muscles burning. Somehow, I'd made it through.

Unfortunately, this was just the first Fundamentals class, and I'd need to take at least seven more of them. I had not anticipated that, since Tuesday hadn't mentioned it, and I was guessing that was on purpose.

I drained the rest of my water and got up after I'd stretched everything out. Tuesday was mobbed with other people in the class asking questions, so I just sat and fiddled on my phone and waited for her to be done.

It took a while, but at last we were the only two people in the room. She came over and plonked down next to me.

"So?" she asked.

"It wasn't horrible," I said. That was the truth. It hadn't been *horrible*. Sure, there had been horrible moments, but overall, I made it through. I'd done some of the movements scaled to the lowest setting, but I'd pushed myself and was proud of what I'd done.

"I'll take that. You did good. Your form is excellent and you take corrections well and apply them. I wish everyone in my classes was like you." For some reason my face got red. That seemed like the highest kind of compliment Tuesday could give me when it came to working out.

"Thank you," I said. "I really didn't know how this was going to go. I was stressing all day."

"You should have told me. I would have reassured you." I gave her a look.

"Would you have? I mean, I tortured you about yoga, it was only fair that you got me back with this." I waved around the room. My stomach made a noise and I knew I needed to eat something ASAP before I went home. Tuesday heard my stomach and got up to grab me a protein bar. She tossed it at me and I managed to catch it. She bit into one and grinned at me.

"I thought I would ease you in. We don't want to scare people, despite what it looks like. Some gyms are high-pressure and want people to push themselves until they throw up, but that's not my goal. I want people to want to come here. I want this to be a safe place where they can push themselves if they want, and accomplish goals, however small. Everyone has a different body, and I want to work with every body. Does that make sense?" It did. It was also my philosophy when it came to yoga. I wanted yoga to be for everyone, and we could modify it to be for everyone.

"I'm not looking forward to my first full workout. And I didn't know that I was committing to eight classes. You forgot to mention that." Tuesday bit into her protein bar.

"You don't have to do all eight. You only promised me one, remember?" That was true.

"How about this? I'll come to all eight classes and you come to six more yoga classes. Then we'll be even." I put my hand out and she shook it.

"Deal. That sounds good. We'll both be stepping out of our comfort zones."

"Yes, but I think you're better at yoga than I'm going to be at lifting weights." I stared at the stack of plates in the corner—they looked menacing.

"You don't have to start out with weight. You can even do it without the bar." I knew that, but I also wanted to prove myself a little. I wanted to prove that my yoga muscles could do something other than yoga.

"And you don't have to do every single hard pose that I suggest. You can do the basic one and I won't think less of you." She made a face.

"Yes, but I don't like doing that. You don't know this about me, but I'm a little competitive." She bumped my shoulder with hers.

"Yeah, no, I got that from reading between the lines of your personality."

We finished our protein bars and then it was time to leave, but I didn't want to.

"So, I know I asked you if you wanted to do dinner and left it kind of open-ended, but do you want to come over tonight? I was going to make a steak stir-fry, if that's something you're into." That sounded amazing right now.

"Let me tell my roommate." I almost never missed dinner with Zee, so that was going to throw a wrench into their dinner plans, but I could just have leftovers tomorrow. I sent them a message that I was going to have dinner with Tuesday, and they wrote me back in all caps that they were mad since they'd already started making dinner, but also that I was going to have to give them full details when I got back.

"I'm good to go," I said, after I answered Zee. Since they practically made all my meals, the least I could do was tell them about my dinner with Tuesday.

"Great. Let me just clean up a little and I'll be ready." She wiped down a few things and organized the equipment. I asked if she needed help, but she said she was fine. I fiddled on my phone and waited. Tuesday turned out the lights and we walked out to the parking lot.

"You can just meet me there. I have a driveway, so you can just park behind me." Wow, lucky. My dream was having a driveway so I didn't have to do street parking ever again.

Tuesday sent me her address and I got in my car.

"Is this a date?" I asked myself, but I didn't know the answer. I didn't want to be a dork and ask Tuesday, but this had all the hallmarks of being a date. Right?

She lived about twenty minutes from the gym, but with traffic it was more like thirty minutes. She beat me there, so I parked behind her car and looked up at the cute building. This was much nicer than where I lived, that was for sure. The neighborhood was everything you'd think a gorgeous Boston neighborhood would be. Brick houses with window boxes, adorable little mini parks and lots of people walking dogs and pushing strollers.

Tuesday buzzed me in, and I walked the narrow stairs to the second floor and knocked on the door.

"It's open," she called, and I walked in, immediately slipping off my shoes. I didn't want to damage the gorgeous hardwood floors. This was an apartment where an adult lived. She had rugs and picture frames and large potted plants on the floor.

"Wow, this is gorgeous," I said, walking into the white and gray kitchen that had little pops of gold and yellow. It was so clean; I didn't want touch anything. Tuesday handed me some wine in a stemless glass.

"Thank you. I've only lived here for a few months. Everything is new because I had to start over." That was news to me.

I swirled my wine around the glass and took a cautious sip. I wasn't used to drinking red wine, but this was lush and sweet. Delicious.

"Why did you have to start over?" I asked, leaning on the white granite countertop. Tuesday paused as she sliced some carrots.

"I'm not sure if I'm ready to talk about that yet. I probably need a few more drinks." She'd changed into a pair of gray sweatpants that hung low on her hips and a tank that showed just a little of her chiseled belly. Her hair was up in a messy bun and, even though I'd seen her in similar clothes before, it was different seeing her barefoot in her house. I still had my clothes on from work and asked if she could show me to the bathroom so I could change. I always had a spare set of regular clothes in my bag so if I wanted to go out spur of the moment, I was covered.

I got distracted on my way to the bathroom by the presence of a giant tank.

"Turtles!" I said, and dashed over. She had quite a setup with fancy lights and lots of fake logs and places for the turtles to rest, and plenty of room for them to swim.

"Hi Percy and Mary," I said as they wiggled around the tank. "Which one is Percy and which one is Mary?" I called to her.

"You won't be able to tell the difference, but I can," she yelled back. I watched the turtles for a few minutes. There was something meditative about seeing them swim around the tank. Then they both got out and sat on one of the rocks in the corner, right under the heat lamp.

"You're cute, but not as cute as the kittens," I whispered before I went to the bathroom to change. When I came back out, Tuesday was throwing steak into a wok.

"Wow, you don't mess around." She turned and looked at me over her shoulder.

"I take food very seriously," she said. I was getting that. She had all kinds of kitchen tools that I had no idea what their purpose was for.

"You should meet my roommate. I think you'd get along really well. They said thank you for the cake, by the way." That cake was almost completely gone. I'd looked for a little bit for breakfast and there was a sliver left. Zee had snuck a bunch of it late last night. Jerk.

"You're both welcome."

"Is there anything I can do? I'm not used to helping because Zee never lets me do anything." Zee had thrown me out of the kitchen on more than one occasion and I was still a little bitter about it.

"No, I've got this," she said, and I huffed.

"No one wants me in the kitchen. Do I give off a bad cooking vibe or something?" Tuesday laughed a little and checked the steak.

"No, I just like doing things the way I like doing things. If you really want to help, you can grab that bowl of vegetables and then toss them in the pan when I tell you to." She cracked a ton of pepper on the steak and the smell was making my mouth fill with saliva.

I stood there with a bowl of carrots, snap peas, bok choy, and broccoli, waiting for my turn. Tuesday threw a bunch of other seasonings in the pan and then pointed at me.

"Ready, set, go," she said, and I threw the vegetables in with gusto. Of course, a few of them jumped ship and landed on the stove.

"Sorry," I said. "I got really excited about vegetables and tossed a little too hard." Tuesday stroked my shoulder.

"It's okay. I'm not mad." I met her eyes and she seemed concerned.

"Sorry, I've just been yelled at a lot in kitchens throughout my life." Thanks restaurateur mom and dad. Tuesday handed me the spatula and motioned for me to stir.

"Are you sure?" I asked. I didn't want to mess this up.

"Absolutely. I need to go get some rice anyway." I stirred the way I'd seen Zee do a thousand times and made sure nothing stuck to the pan or burned. Tuesday came back with a bag of instant rice and threw that in the pan.

"Okay, just a few more things and we're good," she said. "You can keep stirring." I wanted Tuesday to take video of me stirring and send it to Zee to show them that I could do something in the kitchen.

Tuesday threw some fresh herbs in the pan and a few dashes of sauce and then she declared that dinner was done.

"Do you want to just eat on the couch?" I definitely wasn't fancy enough for the lovely dining table that looked like it had been made from reclaimed wood and had a bowl of limes on it that I was pretty sure were fake. It even had a runner on it.

"Yeah, couch sounds good," I said, but then I looked at said couch. It was a light gray color with lots of cute pillows in bright colors. Understated and whimsical at the same time. I liked her style. Also, I was worried about dropping food on the couch and making a stain. I suppose if that happened, I'd just have to create a diversion. Maybe take my shirt off or something. That could work.

I sat down gingerly and put my plate on the coffee table that had a stack of bodybuilding books on it, two remotes, and a candle that smelled like wood smoke. Classy af.

Tuesday handed me a cloth napkin and I placed it on my lap. I wasn't a total cretin; I did know to put my napkin on my lap.

"Should we toast?" she asked, and I held up my wine glass.

"Sure? What should we toast to?" I still didn't know if this was a date or not, and this didn't seem like the best time to ask.

"How about we toast to doing things that scare us?" she suggested, and I liked that.

"To doing things that scare us," I echoed, and we tapped our glasses together and drank.

"Would you mind if I put on some music? Silence makes me uncomfortable sometimes," she said, and I told her to go ahead. "The turtles also like music. They dance in the tank when I play certain songs."

I could believe that. She'd sent me video evidence of it before. They were especially fond of EDM. Instead of that, Tuesday put on a woman singing a folky song with a guitar. I hadn't heard this before, but it was nice.

"This is amazing," I said after my first bite. I didn't know what she had flavored this with, but she must be some kind of sorceress. This stir-fry might put Zee's skills to shame. I should make them do a cook-off and then I could judge the results. That sounded like a fabulous plan.

"Thank you. I got really into cooking after college, right around the same time that I got into weightlifting. I was a little obsessed there for a while, but I like to think I've simmered down with age." I snorted.

"Yeah, because you're so old." Tuesday sipped her wine and then put it down.

"Sometimes I feel like I'm a thousand years old." I asked her what she meant. "I've been through a lot. It's exhausting when I think about it." Right. She had the whole thing with her parents. I had the feeling there was more than that, though.

"Do you want to tell me about it?" She looked into her wine glass as if it was going to give her an answer.

"We'll see. I don't open up easily, Sutton. I've been burned before and it's caused me to be cautious around people. As a result, I've become isolated, but at least when I'm alone, I know who I can trust, and that person is me." Beneath the hard exterior, Tuesday was sheltering a bruised heart. Maybe even a broken one, a heart that had been broken multiple times. This whole time I'd been concerned about getting hurt myself, but now I needed to think about her as well. I couldn't be yet another person who caused her not to trust. The very idea made me feel sick.

"You don't have to talk about anything you don't want to. I understand if it's hard to trust people. I'm not offended or annoyed by that. At all." I stroked her arm and she gave me a tight smile.

"Thanks. That means a lot. I've had people get mad at me before when I couldn't open up, but it's not an easy thing for me to do, at all." I could completely respect that. We'd go at her pace, doing whatever this was that we were doing.

"What made you get into weightlifting?" I said, steering the conversation toward something a little lighter.

"I did it for a girl," Tuesday said, with a wry smile. "If you can believe that."

"I can. I have a long list of things I've done to impress girls. Including, but not limited to: getting a tattoo, skydiving, pretending to enjoy math, pretending to be *bad* at math, and pretending to like a host of things I actually had no interest in. So I get it." I *completely* got it. Tuesday stared at me for a second and then laughed.

"Okay, you win."

"Sorry, I didn't mean to derail your story. Continue." She shook her head and then started again.

"So, I was in college, and there was a girl I had a huge crush on at the gym and she was a lifter. I would be on the treadmill and I'd see her across the room doing squats and overhead presses and I was just in awe of her. After a few weeks I started using the machines near her and hoping she would notice me. Then I started using the weights near her, but that didn't work either. So, I got up my courage and asked her if she would spot me for a bench press, and that finally made her notice me. Her name was Clarity and I was completely in love with her, but she was completely heterosexual, as I came to find out." I winced. Been there, done that.

"But, it sort of worked out because I started weightlifting and met my first real girlfriend doing that, so it turned out okay in the end." I wondered what had happened to that first girlfriend, but I wasn't going to ask. I finished my plate of stir-fry and took it to the kitchen. Tuesday went for seconds.

"I've got some ice cream, if you want. I tend to not keep desserts in the house, except for ice cream, because then I'll just sit and eat them in one sitting. It has happened before after a rough workout." I could imagine. I'd seen her put it away before. Even more than Zee.

Speaking of, I had a few unread messages from them and I checked and they were just wanting updates. So ridiculous, but I knew they just wanted to know because they were happy for me and maybe a little bit because they were living vicariously. They needed a boyfriend, bad. Maybe I could find someone at the gym to set them up with. There had to be at least one decent dude there.

"Everything okay?" Tuesday asked.

"Yup. Just my roommate. They're really supportive and protective at the same time, and you haven't been vetted, so they're curious as to what's going on." There had been people before who hadn't understood my relationship with Zee, and I hoped Tuesday wouldn't be one of those people.

"That's really great you have someone like that in your life," she said after a long time.

"Do you have someone like that?" I asked tentatively.

She sighed and finished her second plate of food and took the plate and napkins to the kitchen instead of answering, which was an answer in itself.

"You're just really lucky." I knew that, which was why I didn't complain too much when Zee ate all the food in the house.

Silence, with the exception of the music and the hum of the filter in the turtle tank, descended on us.

"I would like some ice cream, what flavor?" I asked, following her into the kitchen where she was industriously cleaning the wok.

"Cookie dough brownie," she said, and I thought I was going to pass out. That sounded like the most amazing flavor combination ever.

"Do you have any sprinkles?" I asked. She set the wok down to dry on a dishtowel and opened a cabinet.

"What kind?" She had at least five containers of sprinkles. Sugar, the big chalky ones that they made for different holidays (in this case, hearts for Valentines), the long rainbow sprinkles, the little round ones, and chocolate sprinkles.

"I will take those," I said, pointing to the shaker with the little round multicolored sprinkles.

"Cone?" She asked and I saw she had a lot of those too, and when she opened the fridge, she had chocolate and caramel syrup and whipped cream.

"Did you raid an ice cream stand?" I asked.

"No, I just like to be prepared for sundaes at any moment."

"Were you a Girl Scout?"

"Yup. How did you know? I got a Gold Award and everything." Wow. I'd always wanted to be a Girl Scout, but my parents were too busy to drive me to any of the meetings or events, and I didn't want to ask. They worked so hard and were always so busy that I often didn't ask for anything, even if I was sick, because I didn't want to burden them.

"You get more impressive by the moment, Tuesday," I said.

"Do you want to make your own?" she asked, as she got out the ice cream.

"No, you can do it. I'd like caramel, sprinkles, and whipped cream." Tuesday made up my sundae and then made one for herself, topping it with two waffle cones stuck upside down, chocolate syrup, caramel syrup, two kinds of sprinkles, and whipped cream.

"I don't even care," she said, sticking a spoon into the bowl and then breaking off some of the waffle cone and using it like a chip to scoop up some of the ice cream and toppings.

"Me neither," I said, taking a huge spoonful of my sundae.

We finished eating our sundaes standing up in the kitchen. I was officially full and wanted to curl up on her probably expensive couch and take a nap.

"Thank you for dinner and dessert. That was amazing." Tuesday put the dishes in the dishwasher and then there was nothing left to do.

She rested her arms on the counter and looked up at me.

"Are we doing this?" she asked, clasping her hands together.

"Doing what?" I still had no idea if she would consider this a date or not.

"I don't know," she said, smiling a little. "What are we doing?"

I sighed in frustration. Enough beating around the bush.

"You're attracted to me and I'm attracted to you and we're here at your house and we just had dinner, so I'm guessing, correct me if I'm wrong, that we're dating. Is that way out of line to say?" She stared at me for a second and then laughed.

"Leave it to you to be direct. Yes, I guess we're dating. If you want to put a label on it. I'm not sure that I do. And I'm not sure if I want everyone to know. I'm still . . . I had a breakup that was really bad and I'm still dealing with the aftermath of that." I knew it. I knew there had to be something like that in her past, in addition to her parents passing away. Damn, Tuesday had been through some shit in her life. I wondered if there was more.

"That's fine. We don't have to do anything right now. We can just hang out and make out and see where it goes. You'll come to yoga, I'll go to CrossFit, we'll exchange pictures of our pets and kiss and that's it. Okay?" She inhaled through her nose and stood up.

"Okay." Tuesday walked around the counter to the side that I stood on. "What is all this talk of making out?" Her arms went to my shoulders and she pulled me close. Her breath smelled like sugar and chocolate.

"Did I say making out?" I said, putting my hands on her waist. Anytime I got to touch her it was like an anatomy lesson. An image of Tuesday naked and me with a Sharpie labeling the various muscle groups flashed through my mind. Science had never been so sexy.

"What are you thinking about?" she asked.

"Muscle groups," I blurted out, and she gave me a look. "You have very good muscle groups." That made her throw her head back and laugh. It was a gorgeous, sexy sound, and I vowed that I would hear it at least a thousand times more before I died.

"That is the nicest thing anyone has ever said to me," she said when she was done.

"You're welcome. Now compliment *me*." I batted my eyelashes at her and puckered my lips.

"Do you want to hear what I think about your muscle groups? Or should I show you?" A riot of flutters broke out in my stomach.

"I'll take show over tell at the moment," I said in a choked voice.

"You asked for it," she said. Yes. Yes I had.

Chapter Eleven

Tuesday put a blanket over the turtle tank.

"Should I ask, or . . ." I trailed off as she whispered something to them and then turned to face me.

"I can't have them watching me when we're doing stuff," she said, her cheeks a little red. It was so cute how she blushed sometimes. I wouldn't have picked her for a blusher.

"Good point." I wouldn't want turtles staring at me as I was doing stuff with her either.

"Come here," Tuesday said, crooking her finger at me. I walked over, as if I was on a string she'd tugged. I might as well be. Her eyes were pure blue fire and I was completely captivated.

"You're beautiful, you know that?" she said, reaching up and taking the elastic out of my hair. I put it up when I taught and had forgotten to take it down. My hair tumbled down to my shoulders.

"Am I?" I replied, and then winced at the question.

"Yes, you are."

"Have you seen yourself?" I asked. For some reason, I was afraid to touch her, even though last night she'd been completely pressed against me. Tuesday was more than a little intimidating.

"There aren't a lot of people who would call me beautiful, and I accepted that a long time ago. I'm not here for someone else's consumption." I stared at her.

"What do you mean? You're so fucking hot I can barely remember my own name." Was she serious? If I went out on the street right now and asked twenty people if she was hot, they were all going to say yes. Or else they were wrong, like that one dentist that doesn't recommend a certain brand of toothpaste.

"You think I'm hot?" she asked, putting her arms around my shoulders.

"Ouch," I said, pretending to be hurt.

"What is it?" She pulled her arms back immediately.

"Nothing, you just burned me with your hotness," I said, grabbing her waist and pulling her closer again.

It took her a second to realize what I'd said and then she gave me a wry look.

"Did you seriously just use that line on me?"

"Yes, did it work?" She leaned closer and pressed her forehead to mine.

"Maybe a little."

This time she kissed me, her mouth hot and sweet at the same time. I could taste a hint of the ice cream sundae still on her tongue. She didn't waste any time parting my lips and diving into my mouth, exploring every nook and cranny with a thoroughness that I appreciated. Her tongue thrust against mine, as if she was fucking my mouth and my knees turned to liquid. I didn't know how I was still standing.

Tuesday pulled me down to the couch, as if she'd felt how unsteady I was on my feet.

"You're really good at kissing, you know that?" I told her.

"Thank you. You're not so bad yourself." I wasn't so sure about that, but I did my best. My mind always went blank when it came to kissing. I could have a whole routine planned out with counts and moves and everything, and the second my lips touched another person's, all of that went completely out the window, kind of like right now.

"You're a great kisser, Sutton. Top notch. Thirteen out of ten. Would kiss again." I laughed.

"Can you imagine if there were an app where you rate kisses? That would be horrible." I shuddered at the thought. I was sure that more than a few of my exes would rate me low in the kiss department. That could also possibly be because they were exes and were biased against my kissing ability.

"What on earth are you thinking about, princess?" I shook my head.

"Nothing. Also, why do you call me that?"

Tuesday smiled slowly and then kissed me again.

"How about we talk about that another time. I'd rather put my mouth to use doing something other than talking, yeah?" I agreed. Talking could wait. Kissing now. I answered her by pressing my lips against hers again.

We kissed and we kissed and it was good and warm and sexy and I hadn't been this fucking turned on in at least a few years. Tuesday was the sexiest person I'd ever kissed, hands down. Her hands roamed my body, her fingers dove into my hair and under my clothes. Somehow I found myself lifting my arms so she could pull my shirt over my head. Then my shirt was tossed across the room.

Tuesday ran her hands up and down my front.

"I want to devour you," she said in a low voice.

"Go ahead," I said. Her fingernails scraped my skin just a little. Just enough to leave a little bit of pain behind. My skin rippled with goosebumps.

"Do you want to be devoured here, on the floor, or in the bedroom?" she asked. My mind spun with the possible locations.

"Bedroom," I gasped, and then screamed because I was summarily tossed over her shoulder and carried to said bedroom.

"What are you doing, put me down!" I squealed, and she just laughed and slapped my ass.

"I've been wanting to do this since the first moment I saw you." I was tossed into the center of a California king-sized bed covered by the softest comforter I'd ever felt. I didn't need to check the sheets to know the thread could was high, not that it mattered right now.

Instead, I caught my breath as she climbed on the bed and hovered above me.

"Have you wanted me this whole time? You really didn't act like it. Or did you not want me to know?"

Tuesday huffed above me and didn't answer my question. No, she pulled her shirt off instead, followed by her bra. Seeing her topless rendered me effectively speechless.

"This was the only way to get you to stop talking," she said, shrugging one shoulder.

"It worked," I squeaked. I couldn't think about anything but the sheer perfection of her body. So many muscles and the most perfect set of boobs I'd ever seen. Breasts? Tits? There wasn't really a good sexy word for them. Love globes? Whatever they were, they were perfection. I wanted to put my hands and my mouth all over them. Especially those dark nipples that were pointed right in my direction.

"May I?" I asked, and she sat back on her heels. I pushed myself up until we were almost at the same eye level.

"You're so sexy," I said, as I ran my hands across her collarbone. "You have muscles that I didn't even know existed.

You're like an anatomy chart. If I'd had a picture of you, maybe I would have learned more in biology class." Of course I learned a lot of anatomical terms teaching yoga, but most of the time I didn't remember the complicated names and said things like "shoulders" and "lower back area" instead.

"I'm glad my anatomy pleases you. I didn't know if you'd be into someone like me."

"That's ridiculous." Now it was my turn to decide we'd had enough talking and I stopped it by putting one of her nipples in my mouth. Worked like a charm. She gasped and arched into me, her fingers diving into my hair and digging into my scalp.

I sucked and then flicked the bud with my tongue, listening to her sounds and reading her responses. I wanted whatever was happening to be good for her, and I was going to do my utmost to make that happen.

A moan fell from her lips when I took her nipple between my teeth, so I did it again. Oh yeah, she liked that. I sucked on her nipple and tasted it and teased it until she was begging. Not really sure what she was begging for, but I got the general idea.

"This isn't what I planned when I came over for dinner," I said when I came up for air after taking care of her other nipple.

"Me neither," she said in a breathless voice. "But this is better than the gym floor, don't you think?" It definitely was. Tuesday's bed didn't smell like sweat and tires, and it was a lot softer.

"Absolutely," I said, and she grinned at me.

"My turn."

Once again, I was moving and I wasn't sure how it happened. Tuesday flipped me over onto my back and undid my bra, shoving the straps down my arms and then pulling me up so she could get it off me.

"Oh, I probably should have asked before I ripped that off you, but I figure you would have asked me to stop."

"I mean, I would have if I'd wanted you to. But I didn't." She gazed down at me, and I had to stop myself from crossing my arms over my chest and covering everything.

"You're perfect," she said, brushing her thumbs across my nipples. I gasped and arched into her hands. They were rough and calloused and that added a layer of sensation that made me want to cry, it was so good.

"Do you like that?" she asked, doing it again. I could only make an incoherent sound in response. "I'll take that as a yes."

I nodded my head and then she put her mouth on me and it was the biggest relief because *finally*. I didn't know that I'd been waiting for this, wanting this, and now here we were.

"You're so fucking sweet, Sutton," Tuesday said in a rough voice, as she kissed her way across my chest and up to my neck, sucking on the pulse that pounded there.

Tuesday made a growling noise and pushed me down on my back and straddled my legs. Bracing herself on her arms, her mouth came back to mine. We both still had our bottoms on and, in a fit of boldness, I grabbed the waistband of her sweatpants and started pushing them down her hips. She laughed and pulled back to look down at my face.

"These off," I said, still not able to form a complete sentence.

"Do you want me to take these off?" she asked, her voice playful.

"Yes," I whined. "Pants off."

She held my face in both of her hands.

"You are so fucking cute. I'll take mine off if you take yours off."

That was an even trade. I scrambled out from under her and had my yoga pants off so fast that I busted a few seams. I stood there, completely naked, and waited for her to do the same.

Tuesday froze on the bed, her blue eyes wide as she looked at me. I wasn't going to cover myself this time. The more she looked at me, the more I wanted her to look at me. I wasn't thinking about the little bit of tummy I had, or that one of my boobs was bigger than the other, or that I had a few moles on my chest that I wanted to get taken off.

"What is it?" I asked, and she swallowed audibly.

"You're incredible. Come here." She reached out and pulled me back onto the bed, wrapping her arms around me. The feel of her hot skin against mine was like being burned. She still hadn't taken her sweatpants off.

Tuesday brushed my hair away from my neck and kissed me there, using just the tiniest bit of teeth. I moaned and threw my head back, exposing more of my skin so she could do what she wanted. I was completely at her mercy.

Tuesday bit and kissed her way all down my body, even turning me over to attack my back, which I hadn't thought would be sexy, but holy hell. She left no inch of skin un-kissed or un-licked.

By the time she'd made it near my belly button, I was a trembling, begging mess.

"What do you want?" she asked, pausing and looking up at me. I panted and it took a few seconds for me to find the words I wanted to say.

"Pants off. Touch here." I pointed where I wanted her to touch me. She'd thus far avoided the area, and that made the anticipation all the more intense. My entire body trembled and I couldn't make it stop.

"You're so sweet. Yes, I'll take my pants off." At last, she complied and I almost cried with relief. Tuesday was gorgeous and fit everywhere and I finally had visual confirmation. I wished I had a photographic memory so I could store this image and pull it out when I wanted to remember it.

"I want to lick your entire body," I said, at last forming a complete sentence.

Tuesday chuckled low, a deep sexy sound that went straight to downstairs.

"I think I'd enjoy that very much. Is that what you want?" Maybe later. Right now I was a little too desperate and horny to take my time on something like that. I hoped she wasn't offended.

"I need you," I said, standing up and pressing myself into her. Touching head to toe was intense and electric. I dragged my hands down her front and she shivered, but I didn't think she was cold, since her skin was burning hot.

"You're the sexiest person I've ever seen," I said, finally looking up and meeting those blue eyes. They were liquid blue fire now, melting me from the inside.

"Are you going to lick me all over, Sutton? Or do you want something else?" My mind raced with too many possibilities. I latched on one and said it out loud.

"I want you to sit on my face."

Tuesday was stunned for a second, and then she started to laugh.

"I'm sorry, I'm not laughing at you. I'm laughing at your directness. It's so refreshing. Yes, I can sit on your face. That won't be any hardship on my part." It was a good thing the room was semi-dark because I was blushing up a storm. To distract myself, I reached down and squeezed her ass, both of us making moaning sounds.

"You have the most perfect ass I've ever seen or held." She licked the side of my neck and then looked up at me.

"Have you held a lot of asses?"

"No, not really. But yours is still the best." Walking backwards, I moved us toward the bed and laid back, before scooting myself up on the bed. Tuesday followed me, straddling my hips. Her hair was still up, so she pulled the elastic out of her bun, letting all her thick brown hair fall down her back.

I shook with the need to have her.

"I can't flip you over, but could we switch positions for a little bit?" She nodded and climbed off me, laying out on her back. Now it was my turn to straddle her. Her thighs were so big that I had to really stretch to make it happen. Thank goodness for yoga.

"You're really flexible, aren't you?" Tuesday said, flicking my nipple with one finger, making me yelp.

"Yes, that's one of the many benefits of yoga. I can do all kinds of things with my body." Her eyes widened and I swear her pupils dilated.

"That's the best selling point for yoga I've ever heard." I didn't want to talk about the benefits of yoga right now. Instead of saying anything else, I took one of her nipples into my mouth and then licked my way down her stomach, tracing my tongue through all the dips and valleys and muscles. Tuesday was soft and hard at the same time, and it was the ideal combination.

As I got closer and closer to that place between her thighs, she made more and more noises. I wouldn't have picked Tuesday as noisy in the bedroom, but she surprised me all the time about other things, so why should this be any different?

Her legs twitched and jumped as I bit right near her hipbone.

"Down girl," I said, putting one hand on her.

"I can't help it," she whined, and I got satisfaction from the desperation in her voice. I thought about teasing and tormenting her more, but I didn't have the patience right now.

"Come on," I said, squeezing one of her boobs. I lay next

to her, arranging myself on some pillows. She turned on her side and looked at me.

"Yeah?" she asked.

"Get up here," I said. Moments later, her powerful thighs bracketed my head and I had a full view of Tuesday in all her glory.

"This is the best thing that's ever happened to me," I said, as she trembled above me, a few inches above where I needed her to be. I looked up at her and smiled before grabbing her hips and moving her down just a little as I stuck out my tongue.

"Oh *fuck*," she moaned, as I licked her right down the middle, parting her lips and flicking her clit with my tongue. She tasted like thick honey and salt and I was never going to get enough. I licked her again and again, playing with her clit and her lips and then plunging my tongue inside her, feeling her inner muscles clench. Judging by that, and by the sounds she made, she was close. I squeezed her hips and let her rest her weight more fully on me. I could barely breathe, but that was irrelevant. I sucked hard on her clit and licked her entrance and gave her everything. Her hips rocked, fucking my face, as her sounds increased in volume and intensity. I felt the pulses hit her with my tongue as she rode out her orgasm. It lasted for quite a while, which made me feel a little smug. With one last gasp, she sat back so she was on my upper chest instead, bracing her hands on my thighs.

"Fuck, Sutton," she panted, her eyes sparkling as she looked down at me. She swung her legs over and collapsed beside me.

"That was fucking amazing, holy shit. You're really good at that. Can you breathe? I was afraid I was going to suffocate you." Wow, Tuesday was chatty after sex. At this point I was so turned on, she could probably just breathe in the vicinity of my clit and I would come.

"I'm fine," I said, wiping my hand over my face.

"There's some tissues on the table," she said, pointing. I grabbed a few tissues from the nightstand and wiped my face down. I could still taste her on my skin.

"Good job," she said, patting my arm. "Just give me a minute and then I'm going to fuck the shit out of you." Those were the longest minutes of my life. I was so turned on that it had gotten painful. My labia were hard and I needed to come within the next few seconds or else I might die.

"Please, Tuesday," I said, when I couldn't take it anymore. "Please."

"Are you a little impatient, princess?" she said, rolling on top of me again.

"Yes, are you kidding me?" I was about ready to lose it.

"Well, I have my own plans for you, Sutton. Lay back and enjoy the ride." The second she touched me, I nearly jumped out of my skin. Her fingers lazily traced their way down my chest, stopping briefly to tweak my nipples before she followed their path with her tongue. She hummed softly in appreciation as she reached where I wanted her. Tuesday kissed the perimeter, but didn't go exactly where I needed. I groaned in frustration as she widened my thighs and kissed the inside of each one.

"Someone needs to learn a little patience," she said in a teasing voice.

"This is completely unfair," I said, clenching my hands in the expensive comforter.

"Oh, I think this is completely fair. I think I'll take my time." She traced a circle right around everything and I wanted to scream.

"You said you were going to fuck me, so fuck me," I said, looking down at her. She had her mouth poised just above me and a wicked smile on her face.

"So demanding," she said. "But I guess I've been mean enough."

The second her tongue touched me, I almost cried in relief. Of their own accord, my fingers dove into her hair, pulling her head closer. She chuckled and then plunged one finger inside me, following it closely with a second. Tuesday knew what she was doing, and with a few flicks of her tongue, and a few curls of her fingers, she had stars exploding behind my eyes, and screams coming from my mouth. The orgasm was so powerful that I was sure my heart stopped for a second as my body gave itself over to pure pleasure with no room for anything else. Not even for breathing.

Wave after wave consumed me, until I finally came back down, my body trembling and weak in the aftermath of the storm. A few tears rolled down my cheeks and I wiped them away.

"Thank you," I finally said, and she laughed before coming up to join me again, her face shiny. I handed her the box of tissues.

"You came so fast that I didn't really get to show you my entire repertoire," she said, with a smile on her face. I laughed.

"I'm sure you're very, very good with all of that, you don't have to convince me. I guess I wouldn't be upset if I got to see your entire repertoire, though." That made her laugh and then she put her head on my chest and slung her leg over mine. My hands strayed to her hair, which was a little sweaty.

"Do you want to take a shower?" she asked a few minutes later.

"Sure," I said, and it took me longer to get up than I would have anticipated. I was still completely wrung out from the orgasm.

Tuesday led me into an attached bathroom with a huge

clawfoot tub and a separate shower. I didn't even know they had those in apartments in Boston.

"This is a really nice apartment," I said, as she turned on the water for the shower. I watched as her body moved and shifted, having the benefit of seeing all of it under the bright bathroom lights.

"Your body really is incredible. I was so intimidated by you at first."

"Were you?" she asked, taking my hand and leading me into the shower.

"Yeah, of course."

She put her arms on my shoulders and pulled me under the hot water.

"Are you still intimidated by me?" I nodded.

"Yup. But for different reasons." I shouldn't have said anything because now she was going to ask me about those reasons, and they were tricky, slippery things. Tonight something had shifted, and we'd crossed another bridge that we couldn't turn back from.

And I still wasn't sure that I liked her. Guess you could just have sex without getting completely attached. Go me.

"What are you thinking about?" Tuesday asked, and I turned my attention to her.

"Nothing. Nothing at all." She raised an eyebrow, skeptical, but didn't ask me to elaborate. I kissed her to change the subject and that seemed to work.

The two of us took our time in the shower, soaping each other up and giggling, washing each other's hair and trying not to get soap in our eyes. It was light and fun and the perfect thing to do after the hot-as-hell sex.

Tuesday wrapped me in a robe and we went back out to the living room together. She uncovered the turtle tank and talked to them in a soft voice.

"What are you telling them?" I asked.

"That they're good babies and I'm sorry that I had to ignore them for a little while." Same thing I would have done if we were at my place and I shut the kitties out while we fucked in the bedroom.

"I'm sure they understand."

"I hope so." She joined me back on the couch and I leaned on her shoulder.

"Do you want to stay the night? No pressure, but you could if you wanted to. I mean, we are going to the same place tomorrow." That was a good point, but I missed my kitties and I enjoyed sleeping in my own bed. Staying here seemed like taking things a little too far. All of this was still so new.

"No, that's fine I'll head home in a little while." I could probably fall asleep on this couch right now if I let myself, but I really did need to go home. I got up and brushed my hair out, putting it up so it wasn't wet and on my neck. I got dressed and met her in the living room again.

She looked so beautiful, her hair curling damply, all bundled up in a robe with her cheeks flushed from the sex and the shower. It hit me hard how much I did not want to leave her. No, I wanted to stay and see what it was like to sleep beside her in that big, glorious bed. I'd like to know what she looked like in the morning.

I shook my head at myself and sighed. I didn't tell her how much I wanted to stay; she didn't need to know.

Tuesday got up and came over to me as I stuffed my yoga clothes in my bag and searched for my keys.

"Tonight was amazing. I'm glad you came. How about I bring you breakfast tomorrow? You're going to need a lot of protein." I was still a little sore from the workout, and I knew if I didn't stretch before bed, tomorrow was going to be brutal.

"Thanks, that would be great." I stood there, wondering if

she was going to kiss me. She blinked, fluttering those lashes at me.

"Goodnight," she said in a soft voice, leaning forward to press her lips to mine.

"Goodnight, Tuesday," I said, and then she followed me to the door. It was a gentle end to tumultuous night. I stumbled a little going down the stairs, but I made it to my car in one piece. In a daze, I drove home and floated into my apartment. It was late, but Zee was still awake, probably waiting for me to give them the dirty details.

There they were, sitting on the couch with the sleeping kitties in their lap and the TV on a low volume.

"Well hello there," they said, smirking. "I left you a little bit of cake. I figured you would want it post-coitus." I wanted to throw a pillow at them for using the word "coitus." Instead, I went to the kitchen and got the last piece of cake and put it on a plate.

"It's really weird how invested in my sex life you are, Zee," I said, as I took my first bite. The sugar went right to my system. It didn't matter because I was going to be up late anyway, thinking about might night with Tuesday. Had that really happened?

"I just care about you and your sexual health. Orgasms are good for you." I made a face at them.

"Seriously, ew."

"Fine, fine. But how did things go otherwise? You don't have to tell me about the sex parts, if there were any sex parts." I giggled.

"Sex parts," I repeated.

"Tell meeeee," they whined, and woke up the kitties. I pulled them into my lap instead.

"She made me dinner and we had ice cream sundaes. The whole thing had a bit of a surreal quality to it. I'm still not really sure that it happened, because holy shit, Zee. Just a few weeks ago I was annoyed as fuck at her and now . . ." I trailed off.

"Now?" Zee said, motioning for me to elaborate.

"Now everything has changed." That was the bottom line: everything had changed and I wasn't standing on solid ground anymore. The earth beneath my feet had fractured, and I was trying to stay upright and not fall into the unknown.

"You okay?" Zee asked, putting a hand on my shoulder.

"Yeah, my life just got a whole lot more complicated and I don't know if I'm excited or terrified." Zee laughed.

"All the best things in life are equal parts exciting and terrifying." They had that right.

"I don't know," I whined, shoving my face into a pillow.

"You're going to be fine. And you can always talk to me about it if you want. Or not talk to me about it. Either way, I know she makes you happy, doesn't she?"

"I think she does? I guess I can't get over my initial feelings about her. I go with my gut when it comes to people, and I still have those feelings lingering along with the new feelings and now I have too many feelings, Zee. Please help me get rid of my feelings." I finished my slice of cake and was suddenly so tired that I didn't know if I was going to make it to my bed.

"I can't, my dear friend. You've got to deal with them on your own." I groaned and then pouted.

"I don't want to."

Zee laughed and got up.

"On that note, I'm heading to bed. Unless you want me to stay up with you for a little while? I have an early meeting tomorrow." It was seriously late and I wanted to ask them to stay up with me, but I needed to go to bed. I had a full day tomorrow, as well as my second CrossFit class.

"No, it's fine. I'm going to bed too." I levered myself off

the couch and put my plate in the dishwasher before picking up the kittens and taking them to bed with me. I rolled out my home yoga mat and did a quick flow, focusing on stretching my tired muscles so I wouldn't be as sore in the morning.

Piling the kittens in bed, I turned on the TV to lull me to sleep. My body was exhausted, but my brain was still going, thinking about tonight.

I swear I could still taste her on my lips.

"Fuck," I said, and closed my eyes. I could still see echoes of her gorgeous body, and hear the sounds she made when she came. I was never going to forget tonight. Ever.

I was going to have to take each day as it came and wait to see what happened next. All I knew was that I wanted Tuesday again and again and again. I wanted her so much it made my skin ache and my teeth clench at the thought of being with her again.

I should have stayed the night with her. My bed was so empty.

Chapter Twelve

TUESDAY MESSAGED ME the next morning and asked what I wanted for breakfast. I put in my order with a smile on my face, and then winced as I got out of bed. Yup, I was sore. I'd hoped I wouldn't be, but here I was. It was like going back to the days when I was doing my teacher training and taking multiple classes a day. I hadn't done that much in years, and I felt a little guilty about it.

I told Zee I was having breakfast with Tuesday, and I hoped they weren't bummed since they always cooked breakfast for me. I was ravenous by the time I made it to the studio, but Tuesday was there at the top of the stairs waiting for me with food. I'd never seen anything that sexy or delicious, and I wasn't just talking about the bags of food and coffee she held.

I wanted to eat the food and then eat her, right on these steps. I swallowed and tried to put a cork in my lust, at least until we weren't at work.

"Thank you," I said, taking the bag from her. I didn't know if I was allowed to kiss her since no one else was around, so I didn't.

"Hey, come here," she said, as I set the bag on the bench by the door so I could take off my street shoes.

"What?" I said, looking up at her.

"Where's my kiss?" she said, pushing her bottom lip out in the most adorable pout I'd ever seen.

"I didn't know if we were doing that kind of thing. I don't know the rules, Tuesday." She sat down next to me.

"You're right. We haven't set parameters. So how about we do that right now?" I took the coffee cup and inhaled deeply of the hazelnut latte.

"I need caffeine first."

I had pretty much drained my coffee and Tuesday had eaten two sandwiches by the time I was ready to talk about rules for our relationship.

"Okay. Let's do this." I cracked my neck and she gave me a funny look.

"You look like you're preparing for a workout, not a conversation," she said. Feeling silly, I got up and started breathing heavily and doing exaggerated stretches and grunting.

"Now you're just being ridiculous," Tuesday said, but she was trying—and failing—to hide a smile. Ha.

I sat back down next to her.

"Okay, serious time. What are the parameters of our relationship?" I'd wanted them from the beginning, but now that we were talking about them, I wanted to run away and hide under a pile of yoga mats.

"I think when we're alone, kissing is entirely allowed and encouraged, at least on my side." I nodded, agreeing with that.

"Yes, kissing should definitely be a priority. What about when people are around? I don't want to only kiss in secret." Tuesday sighed.

"Can you give me maybe a week to adjust to all this before

we go public? I'm still trying to wrap my brain around all of this." She gestured between us.

"Yeah, same here." A week seemed completely fair, so I agreed to that. "What else?"

She thought about that for a minute.

"You have an open invitation to spend the night at my apartment whenever you'd like." That was surprising.

"Whenever I'd like, huh?" I said, stroking my chin. Tuesday's eyes narrowed.

"Within reason," she added.

"Oh, that's no fun." She hit me lightly on the shoulder. "Okay, fine. You're also welcome at my place, but I don't know if you want to deal with my roommate constantly asking you probing questions and two kittens that will die without constant attention." Tuesday shrugged one shoulder.

"I think I can handle both of those things."

"You seem awfully confident about that," I said. Tuesday hadn't experienced the entirety of Zee, and I was dying to see how that first interaction was going to go.

I finished my own sandwich, as well as a small cup of fruit. I was already wired from the caffeine. Teaching today was going to be interesting.

"Look, I should get downstairs, I have to get ready for my first session, but do you want to get lunch later?" she asked. I shook my head.

"Can't today. I teach the noon class, so no lunch for me. I'm just going to live on kombucha and almonds today." Tuesday stood up.

"No, that's not acceptable. I'll bring you something. So I guess I'll see you at seven?" Ugh, I didn't want to think about another CrossFit workout right now. It was far too early.

"Yup, can't wait," I said, giving her a week smile.

"You'll be fine." She patted my shoulder and then kissed

my cheek. I pointed to my lips with one finger and she laughed before she pressed a quick kiss to my lips. That wasn't enough for me, so I grabbed her shirt and kissed her more thoroughly until my head spun.

"Stop that," she said into my mouth. "If you keep kissing me like that, we're never going to get any work done."

"Oh well," I said, trying to kiss her again, but she dove away and pointed at me.

"You stay there. I'm going downstairs. I'll see you later." I grumbled, but let her go. It was good she left because, not two minutes later, my first student came up the stairs. He was early, but it was a reminder that Tuesday and I were surrounded by people most of the time.

I tried to get my mind on teaching, so I went to check the room and get the heat started, but all I could think about was the dirty, delicious things I was going to do to her tonight.

I SENT Zee a message that I was going over to Tuesday's again and they sent back a pouting emoji, but also told me to have a good time. They really did need to get a boyfriend. Then I wouldn't feel so guilty about spending so much time away from them. I didn't want to be the kind of friend who would toss their BFF away when they got into a romantic relationship. Zee and I had been through too much to let that happen.

I'd never had an issue choosing a relationship over Zee, but then again, I'd never been in a relationship that felt like this. This thing with Tuesday . . .

If I thought about it too much, it scared the absolute shit out of me. We'd been together for only a few days, but it felt like so much longer. I'd never been in a relationship that moved this fast. I'd also never been in a relationship with anyone like Tuesday, so there was that as well.

She brought me lunch in the middle of the day, and I didn't even have a chance to thank her for it because I was on the phone dealing with a customer account issue. She left it on the desk and gave me a little wave before going back downstairs.

I got off the phone and devoured the chicken wrap and chopped salad in less than two minutes. I sent her a kissy face video to thank her. The rest of the day was go, go, go and I was almost looking forward to CrossFit because at least I wouldn't have to think while I was doing it. I'd only have to worry about the next rep, and my arms and legs not giving out on me. Fun times.

At last, it was seven and I said goodnight to Priya and went downstairs. A few of the same people were there and this time I tried to make conversation. The tiny woman next to me who didn't look like she could lift a kitten, let alone a barbell, was Victoria, and she was doing this because she wanted to be able to open spaghetti jars and not always have to ask her boyfriend. A worthy goal, I told her. There was also Chloe, who was here because her wife, Dimple, who was much more into CrossFit than Chloe and she'd wanted to have a hobby they could do together.

"I hope I don't die. I just don't want to die or hurt myself," Chloe said, looking at the equipment as if it was going to leap out and bite her.

"You could come upstairs and do yoga. I run Breathe Yoga. I can't guarantee you won't hurt yourself, because that's always a risk, but I can guarantee you won't die." She laughed and said she might take me up on that.

"Hey, no stealing my customers," Tuesday said from across the room, pointing at me.

"I'm networking, hush," I said, waving her off. Chloe and Victoria gave me looks.

"Are you two friends?" Victoria asked.

"Something like that," I said, trying not to smile. Very special friends.

Tuesday started the class and we went through learning the moves again, followed by another brutal workout. There were pull-ups. There were burpees. I wanted to throw up and cry and beg her to kill me at the same time but, somehow, the clock ran down and I made it through four rounds of the awful.

"Good job," Tuesday said to me, as I gasped and tried not to sob on the floor. Sweat kept running into my eyes so I just shut them and prayed for death. I felt someone sit next to me.

"Do you hate me now?" Tuesday asked, and I cracked my eyes open.

"Maybe," I said. "You'd better make up for this and I have several suggestions of how you can do that."

Tuesday smirked.

"Oh, really? Several? I'm guessing none of them involve clothing." She whispered the last part so no one could hear, even though the music was loud.

"Nope. None of them do." I sat up and winced. "That was way worse than the first night, you monster." Tuesday stood up and held her hand out to me.

"Come on, you need to stretch so you don't seize up. Then it will be way worse tomorrow." I knew she was right, but I also knew that I didn't want to move.

"Come on, you can do it." I groaned as I got to my feet and then did a forward fold before struggling back to a downward- facing dog and then child's pose. I added a few more stretches and then looked up at her.

"Satisfied?" I said.

"Not yet," she said. "But I'm guessing you'll take care of that later." If I could move later.

I crawled toward my phone and checked out my social media before going to the bathroom to mop my face off. I definitely needed a shower before any kind of sex tonight. I was a mess, and not a cute one.

When I came out, everyone was gone and Tuesday was cleaning up.

"I'm disgusting," I said, pulling my drenched shirt away from my boobs.

"You can shower here if you want. Or shower back at my place. I'll get you all nice and clean and then really, *really* dirty." If my knees hadn't been trembling from the workout, they were now. I had to grip onto the wall so I didn't completely collapse.

"Will there be food as well?" Tuesday laughed and kissed me on my sweaty cheek.

"Yeah, there will be food. There's always food at my house."

We took our separate cars, which was nice because then I didn't have the pressure of having to stay the night. I still wasn't sure if I was ready for that. Like Tuesday, I needed at least a week to adjust to everything.

When I got to her apartment, I mumbled that I was going right for the shower. I'd brought an extra outfit, as well as some pajamas, just in case I'd need them.

The shower was wonderful, and I made all kinds of indecent noises that Tuesday could probably hear from the kitchen. I toweled my hair off as I walked into the kitchen to find Tuesday making curry chicken with rice.

"This smells fucking amazing, holy shit," I said, inhaling deeply. Tuesday really did need to compete with Zee for title of Best Cook.

"We also have a side salad, and I restocked my ice cream, so there's that as well." If I hadn't had to go through that brutal workout, tonight would have been perfect. My body had already started to ache and I asked Tuesday where the pain meds were and she directed me to the medicine cabinet in the bathroom.

I made faces at the turtles as Tuesday cooked. I didn't feel like helping tonight. She brought plates over and we sat on the couch together and she put on some soft violin music.

"This is really nice, thank you," I said, as I dug my fork into the deliciousness. "I feel completely spoiled."

"You're welcome. It's nice to have someone to cook for. I'm used to it just being me, and I had to adjust to cook for one instead of two." I decided to probe a little about that.

"When did your last relationship end?"

"Less than a year. It was . . . it was bad. Real bad." Her face fell and she looked down at her plate as her lower lip trembled. But then she took a deep breath through her nose and looked up.

"I'm dealing with it. Sort of." She let out a self-deprecating chuckle.

"That's the way I always handled breakups. Although, I was never really bummed when we broke up and it was almost always a mutual decision." I shoved a giant forkful of food into my mouth. Holy shit, this was good. Plate-licking good.

"You're lucky. You've never had your heart broken?" I felt a little guilty saying yes.

"It's not for lack of trying. I had every intention of falling in love with all of them, and then it just didn't happen. I just couldn't get there." I laughed, but it was a real fear that I had. A fear that I had never voiced before and was shocked that I'd said it now in front of Tuesday. I blamed the workout for weakening my defenses and loosening my tongue.

"Maybe you just weren't dating the right people. Or maybe you don't experience that kind of attraction." I'd thought about that, but I didn't think it was the case. I was the kind of person who didn't love easily, but when I did, I was all in. At least I thought I would be, when I got to that point.

"What happened with your ex?" I asked, to turn the attention away from me for a little while. Tuesday told me a little about her breakup.

"She was supposed to be my business partner as well, so that really fucking sucked. I had to dissolve all these contracts and everything. That's why I'm the only one running the gym. I was supposed to be doing the coaching side, and she was going to handle the business. So listen to my advice and say to never get your romantic relationships involved in your business. Ever." Yeah, she'd definitely had gotten burned, but my parents made it work and I told her that.

"I'm not saying it can't work, I'm just saying that the consequences when it doesn't work are dire." For some reason, the way she said the word "dire" was hilarious.

I giggled and finished my first plate and then attacked my salad with my fork.

"What's funny?" Tuesday asked.

"Nothing. The word 'dire' is hilarious." I kept saying it and laughing.

"I think you've got the post-workout sillies," Tuesday said, trying not to laugh at me.

"I'm sorry," I said, wiping the tears from my eyes. "I don't know what came over me."

Tuesday stared at me with a hint of a smile on her face.

"You're so cute, you know."

"Am I?" I asked.

"Yeah, you are." I finished my salad and she didn't talk any more about her ex, which was probably a good thing. I didn't want to know or think about her past relationships, and I didn't want to think about mine either. They weren't relevant right now. It was just the two of us and the turtles.

"I really want to meet the kittens," she said, as she finished her first plate and then went for a second. I handed her mine and asked for more as well. That workout had left me famished.

"You can come over this weekend, if you want. Zee might be there and you can finally meet them. I'm sorry in advance." Tuesday returned with the plates and we made weekend plans. I had to teach the first half of the day, so we decided to have dinner out and then go back to my place.

"And you can stay the night if you want. If you don't mind sharing the bed with me and two kittens. It's not as big and nice as yours." Compared to her apartment, mine was a shithole and I hoped she didn't judge me for it. Clearly, she had money, but I didn't begrudge her that because at least I had living parents. We didn't talk much, and they hadn't wanted me in the family businesses (for whatever reason), but they were alive and I knew they loved me. If I ever got into a situation where I couldn't pay my rent at the studio, they would bail me out. I was very, very lucky that way.

"That's okay. I don't mind being cozy with you. I miss a lot of the stuff from my old apartment, but I had to leave it behind when I broke up with my ex. It was better to start over." I got that, completely.

We finished our second plates of food and then topped it off with ice cream. By that time I was so tired, I could barely keep my eyes open. I wanted sex, but my body was saying no.

"I'm sorry," I said through a yawn. "I really do want to do wicked things to you, but then you made me work out. You only have yourself to blame for this situation." I yawned again and my eyes flickered closed.

Tuesday moved over to me on the couch and put my head on her shoulder.

"We can snuggle. I don't have any expectations when it comes to sex, Sutton. I'm happy to have you right here." I sighed and she played with my damp hair.

"Do you want to watch a movie or something?"

I nodded and she picked up the remote to choose something. It was like the last time we'd tried to pick something to watch where we couldn't agree on anything but documentaries. This time it was one about Multi-Level Marketing scams, which was right up my alley. I snuggled into Tuesday and her glorious arms went around me. My fingers softly scratched her forearm and she made little encouraging sounds and tilted her arm for more.

This. This was what I had been wanting all those nights when I went to bed alone. Even more so than the sex, this is what I had been craving for so long. This closeness, this intimacy. Just this.

Of course, my body was so exhausted, that about fifteen minutes later my eyes were too heavy to hold open and so I closed them for what I told myself was just a few seconds.

"Are you awake?" a voice said, and I slowly swam back to consciousness. The movie was over and Tuesday was tapping my shoulder.

"Uh huh," I mumbled. "Totally awake."

"You are not. Come on. Time for bed."

"No, no," I weakly protested, as she somehow picked me up and stood at the same time. "I'm fine."

"You don't have to stay the night, but you need a nap at least. Come on, princess." This time the nickname had a soft edge to it that caused little flutters in my stomach.

I tried to protest, but she tucked me into her bed and it was so soft and so cozy that I couldn't fight anymore. I gave up and sighed as I let myself give in to sleep again.

∼

THE NEXT TIME I woke up, I wasn't alone and it was morning. Oops? I turned and found Tuesday slumbering next to me, the blankets clutched in her hands around her face. I had to pee like hell, but I also just lay there for a moment and stared at her. How had I ended up in bed with this hot, mean goddess?

As if she had heard my thoughts, her eyes opened. She blinked a few times and then smiled as she found me watching her.

"Were you watching me sleep like a weirdo?" she asked in a sleepy voice, stretching her arms over her head.

"Just a tiny bit," I said. "I guess I stayed the night, huh?" She yawned and nodded.

"Yup. I was going to wake you up again and have you go home, but you were out. I couldn't have gotten you out of here if I tried." I tossed the covers back and winced as I put my feet on the floor and hobbled to the bathroom. We weren't at the "leave the door open while you pee" stage of our relationship yet (I didn't think), so I closed the door and did what I needed to do, and then came back to find her sitting up in bed, her hair adorably rumpled and her eyes just a tiny bit puffy. I'd wondered what she looked like in the morning and now I knew. All I wanted to do was kiss her, so I went back over and gave her a closed-lip kiss.

"My mouth is gross," I said, but she pulled me back and kissed me fully.

"I don't care." I wasn't so sure of that, but I took her word for it and kissed her back before running back to the bathroom and realizing I didn't have a toothbrush here.

"Here," Tuesday said, handing me an extra brush head for her electric toothbrush. "You can use mine." She even had a fancy toothbrush. This place was better than a hotel.

I brushed my teeth with her toothbrush and then flossed.

"Are you going to sit there and watch me?" I asked, as she sat on the tub.

"Maybe," she said. "It's strange seeing you here, but I think I like it."

"You definitely have better floss than I do. And a nicer toothbrush." I wiped my face on a towel and turned around to face her.

"My turn." She did the same routine and I had to admit, it was nice sharing this kind of intimacy. I had never lived with anyone I'd been seeing, so I hadn't gotten much of this kind of thing. For a moment, I entertained what it would be like living with Tuesday.

Absurd, I knew. We hadn't even been dating a week. Still, the image of coming home and seeing her in the kitchen talking to the kittens as she cooked was hard to shake.

I was definitely putting the sex before the horse and I needed to slow the fuck down.

TUESDAY HAD MESSAGED Zee from my phone letting them know that I had fallen asleep at her place so they wouldn't worry, and I had a slew of messages asking for updates from Zee when I checked it.

"They seem great, I can't wait to meet them," she said, as I went through the messages and tried to respond to them all. I also had missed an entire discussion on the group chat about hot sauce, religion, and Elvis that I wanted to catch up on, but I needed to get to the studio. My hair was a chaotic mess from being slept on while it was still damp, so I put it up and called it good.

"It's a good thing I keep extra clothes in my bag, in my car, and at the studio. My tendency to spill things on myself has paid off, finally." Tuesday handed me a cup of coffee with creamer in it.

"Bless you," I said, taking it from her. This was going to be a four-cup kind of day.

"I can make something if you want. I've got tons of stuff." Watching her cook might make me a little late, but I decided the risk was worth it.

"Sure."

Tuesday made bacon, eggs, and avocado toast while I drained my coffee and went for a second cup. I inhaled the food and then rushed out the door, saying I would see her in a little while. I got lucky and traffic wasn't too bad, so I made it to the studio on time.

I couldn't stop smiling, even though my body was sore as fuck after the workout last night, and I had another one to look forward to tonight. Joy. How was I going to make it through this week? At least I'd had an awesome night of sleep at Tuesday's. I needed to do that more often, even though I'd missed the kitties terribly and begged Zee to send me some pictures of them and give me an update on their night. I hoped they didn't think I'd abandoned them.

The rest of my day was a struggle between thinking about Tuesday, wondering what she was doing, worrying about the workout tonight, being sore from the one from last night, and trying to juggle running my business. Of course, there were a million voicemails and customer issues and our website crashed. I wanted to sit and cry, but I had to handle it. There was no one else. I did send a panicked message to Ellen, asking if she could come in and teach one of my classes so I could deal with the other shit. She said that she could and I promised that she was my favorite person in the history of the world, but she called my bluff. I thanked her profusely again and got back to my massive to-do list.

I didn't have time for lunch again, and somehow it appeared outside my office door. Tuesday again.

Somehow I made it to seven, and dragged myself to the workout. It was nice to see Victoria and Chloe again, and we compared our muscle soreness in solidarity. This time there was no Tuesday teasing. She got right down to business and I wanted to start crying when she explained the workout.

This was going to be rough.

Chapter Thirteen

Somehow, I made it through the workout, and the next, and then it was the weekend. I told Zee that Tuesday was coming over after dinner to hang out with me on Saturday, and they said that they already had plans so we could have the house to ourselves. I had suspicions that they'd made plans for that eventuality, but when I asked them, they said that they'd had this event planned for weeks.

"But I'll see you on my way out. I really do want to meet her." I wasn't sure how that was going to go, but I had to get to work, so I decided not to worry about it too much. That plan backfired, because I couldn't tell my brain not to worry. It did whatever the fuck it wanted without my input most of the time.

I'd put on one of my favorite striped casual jumpsuits and left my hair down. When she came to the door, her eyes went wide. She'd mostly seen me in yoga clothes, so I'd wanted to knock her socks off.

"Wow. You look amazing," she said. I was also stunned, because she had on a pair of jeans that were so tight they looked like they would rip if she tried to take them off, and a top that showed off her arms in the best way. I was stupefied for a moment.

"*You* look amazing, holy shit, Tuesday. Can I see the back view?" She rolled her eyes, but spun, and I stopped her from turning all the way around.

"Let me get a good look at the back view. Uh huh. Yup. That's definitely working for me." Those jeans didn't have to do her ass any favors because it was already the greatest ass in the universe, but still, it was nice to see clothing hugging her like that.

"Can I turn around now?" she asked, looking over her shoulder.

"Just give me one more second." I tilted my head and sighed happily.

"I'm hungry," she whined.

"Fine, fine. But I want to stare at you later." I gave her butt one little smack and she yelped before turning around.

"No spanking in public," she said, pointing at me.

"But not no spanking? Just not in public?" There was a hopeful lilt to my voice. Tuesday tried to fight a smile and lost the battle.

"Let's talk about that later." I rubbed my hands together in glee and she pushed me toward the stairs.

∼

WE WENT to a nicer Italian place for dinner and I got a plate of pasta that was half my body weight, which I devoured. Tuesday ate an entire pizza and a serving of meatballs. The waiter came over to ask us about dessert, saw the empty plates and almost fainted.

"Yes, we want dessert," Tuesday said, reaching for the

menu in his hand. He gave it to her and took the empty plates, shaking his head.

We ordered a limoncello cheesecake and a double chocolate cake since we couldn't decide which we wanted more.

After the dessert plates had been scraped clean, I sat back and put my hands on my belly.

"That was fabulous. We should definitely come here again."

"Yeah?" Tuesday said, resting her elbow on the table and her chin in her hand.

"Definitely. We can try something else on our next date." Tuesday laughed softly.

"I still can't believe we're dating." I reached my hand across the table and she took it, twisting our fingers together.

"I know, but I've gotta say that I like dating more than I like not dating you. Even if I don't like you." I said the last part playfully, so she would know I was joking.

"I don't like you either," she said, but her eyes were smiling.

This time I got the check and then we left, our hands still wrapped together.

∼

I THOUGHT about giving Tuesday instructions and rules for meeting Zee, but then I decided that was ridiculous and it would be fine. I wanted them to like each other so much, I could barely deal. The closer we got to my apartment, the more nervous I got. Tuesday put her hand on my leg.

"If they're as great as you say they are, then I'm going to like them. Stop stressing." I couldn't. Zee was on the couch when we walked into the house and got up to come over and shake Tuesday's hand.

"It's so nice to finally meet you. I feel like I know you

already," Zee said, and I could tell they were genuinely happy to see us.

Tuesday shook Zee's hand, and said "likewise." There was one of those moments of silence and then it was broken by the sounds of small kittens.

"Oh my goodness," Tuesday said, in a tone of voice I'd never heard. Not even with the turtles. She leaned down and picked both of them up, cradling them to her chest as they purred and pawed at her clothes and hair.

"Aren't you the most precious things in the entire world?" She kissed both of their heads and rocked back and forth with them, like they were fussy human babies.

"She likes kittens and she gave us cake. I'd say she's a winner so far," Zee said with a grin. Tuesday looked up from the kitty faces, as if she'd forgotten anyone else was in the room.

"Sorry. I've just seen so many videos of them that I've been thinking about this for ages." That made Zee laugh and Tuesday's face got red. "Sorry. Not that I wasn't excited about meeting you." Tuesday looked at me to throw her a line.

"It's fine, Zee is just messing with you. If you didn't fall in love with the kittens, they'd be concerned. Right?" I turned to Zee for confirmation.

"Exactly."

We sat down on the couch and Tuesday put the kittens down on the floor.

"So, I hear you do CrossFit," Zee said, and I gave them a warning glance.

"Yes?" Tuesday said, not sure what was going to follow that statement.

"I hear that's a really good workout. I'm more into active sports, but I can appreciate the competitive aspects." I stared at Zee. They had pulled no punches when they'd told me how much they despised that kind of CrossFit environment before. One of the things I'd been worried about was Zee attacking Tuesday for being involved in it, but here they were, surprising me.

"It is competitive, if you want it to be." Once Tuesday got talking about CrossFit, she didn't want to stop, much like I was with yoga. Zee was used to being around passionate people, and was passionate themselves, so this was nothing new.

Zee asked Tuesday some more questions about the gym and then they talked turtles for a few minutes before Zee's phone went off.

"That's my ride."

"Where are you going?" I asked. They'd been a little cagey about what these "plans" were.

"Nowhere," they said, getting up and patting me on the head.

"Seriously? Where are you going and who are you going with?" I called behind them as they ran out the door.

"None of your business, Mom!" they yelled over their shoulder and then closed the door.

"I bet they're going on a date, but I don't know why they wouldn't tell me about it. They always want to know every single detail of what my romantic relationships are." I rushed to the window, but the car that picked Zee up was already gone.

"Dammit. I bet they're on a date." That was going to bug me for the rest of the evening. I sent them an accusatory message, but they didn't respond right away.

"You two are really close, aren't you?" Tuesday commented from the couch.

"Yeah, I can't imagine my life without them. They're the closest thing I've ever had to a sibling. We were randomly paired up in college and we've lived together ever since. I think part of my reluctance to get into a completely committed relationship is that I don't want to not live with Zee. I think if someday we could have separate homes that were still attached in some way, that would be ideal." Zee and I would always be together somehow. I hoped Tuesday was okay with that. Some people wouldn't be.

"That's great that you found each other and that you've stayed so close. I'm envious, to be honest," she said, stroking both of the kittens heads at once.

"It doesn't weird you out that we're so close?" That was always my concern.

"No? Should it?" I breathed a sigh of relief.

"No," I said. "Would you like the grand tour?" She stood up and carried the kittens with us as I showed her the apartment.

"Do you want some coffee or anything?"

"Maybe some tea, if you have it." I had tons of tea, and I opened the cabinet in the kitchen and showed her my bounty.

"Pick your poison." She pointed to a box of peppermint, and I brewed two cups in the kettle. When it was just me, I always just put the water in the microwave.

"This is nice," she said about the kitchen.

"Not as nice as yours," I mumbled.

"What?" she said.

"Nothing. Do you want honey or lemon?"

"Both."

We took our tea back into the living room and curled up together on the couch.

"It's nice being here with you," she said, turning her face and kissing my lips softly.

"It's nice having you here," I said, and moved so I could kiss her more easily. Unfortunately, there were two little fuzz balls that protested me doing that.

"Don't be clitblockers," I scolded them in a soft voice, before setting them on the floor. I looked up to find Tuesday choking on her tea and coughing.

"You okay?" She wiped her mouth with a napkin and nodded, taking a few deep breaths.

"Clitblockers? Really?" I shrugged.

"I mean, where is the lie?" Tuesday smiled and shook her head.

"What made you think you're getting laid tonight?" Her tone was flirtatious.

"Um, because you can't resist me?" I posed dramatically, throwing my head back and then shaking my boobs.

"You're a little cocky, aren't you?"

"No, I'm a little clitty," I pointed out. That made her laugh again.

Tuesday leaned closer and used my shirt to pull my mouth to hers.

"You're a little everything, princess," she said in a low voice, and I shivered with goosebumps.

"Is that good?" I asked. I hoped it was good.

"Mmm, very good." Our lips met again and she tasted of mint and honey and I was starved for her. I immediately climbed in her lap and started to go for her clothes.

"Wait, wait," she said, grabbing my hands to stop me. "I can't do this in front of them." I was confused.

"In front of who?"

"Them," she said, pointing to the kittens who sat on the floor and stared at us, unblinking. It was eerie.

"Okay, I think we need to move this somewhere else." I got off of Tuesday's lap and went to the pantry where I hid some of their catnip-filled toys. That was one way to keep them distracted for a little while.

I shook the toys at them and they knew immediately what they were and started pawing my legs and crying.

"Yes, I know. Here you go." I set the toys down and they both pounced, meowing happily. "There, now we can do whatever we want. That will amuse them for at least a little while." I looked up at Tuesday with a grin.

"Well then," she said, getting up from the couch. "What are we waiting for?"

∽

I LED the way to my bedroom, grateful that I'd cleaned it last night in preparation for her being here. It hadn't been this tidy since I'd moved in. Not that I was a slob, but I had a demanding job that required a lot of hours, and that didn't leave a whole lot of energy for cleaning. I also had two kitties that were constantly getting into mischief and pulling things out of drawers.

My room was small, but I liked to think it had a comfortable, unassuming vibe. No high thread-count sheets here.

Tuesday shut the door and rested her back on it.

"Come here," she said, crooking her finger at me.

"No, you come here," I said, going over to sit on the bed. "We're on my turf."

"You're being awfully bossy, princess," she said.

"Yup. My room, my rules." I reached my arms out for her and she crossed the room and came to stand in front of me. "Now, turn around and show me that butt." She burst out laughing, but spun around and then did something that almost made me slide off the bed.

Tuesday bent over and did something to make her ass undulate in the way I'd only seen people do in music videos.

"That's a very impressive skill, you should put that on your resume," I said, when I could remember how to talk. My voice sounded a little strangled and breathless.

"Thanks, I'll remember to do that," she said, looking at me over her shoulder.

"But you know what would make that even better?" I asked, reaching out and grabbing the waist of her pants and tugging her in between my legs.

"What?" she said, squealing a little.

"If you were wearing *no* pants while doing that." I tugged at the waistband again.

Tuesday gasped.

"Are you trying to get my pants off?"

"Yes? I thought that was obvious. If my choices are Tuesday with pants and Tuesday without pants, I'll take the second, every time." Tuesday laughed and I heard the sound of a zipper.

"In that case . . ." In a feat that could only be described as magic, Tuesday removed the skintight jeans and discarded them on my floor. They looked so much better that way. She was left in underwear that was more of a whisper than actual fabric.

"I didn't know people actually wore thongs," I said. "Isn't it like having floss between your cheeks?" I stroked the little tail of fabric that rested above her ass.

"You certainly have a way with words. And you get used to it," she said, spinning around and taking my cheeks in both hands and tilting my face up.

"Should I shake my ass again?" What kind of a question was that? The answer would always be yes. I held up a finger for her to wait a second and grabbed my phone, scrambling to find the right song.

"Okay, got it," I said, hitting play. Tuesday groaned, but

then bent over and started shaking her ass in time with the music.

"I'm not doing this all night," she said.

"Mmm, just a few more seconds," I said, tilting my head to get the best view. "Can you teach me how to do that?"

"Sure," she said, doing a little twirl. The front of her thong was completely transparent and I was starting to see the benefit of them.

"Now, you dance for me," she said, taking my hands and pulling me to my feet.

"So, I know I know how to do a yoga flow, but, uh, I'm not super coordinated when it comes to dancing. I'm guessing any kinds of moves I'm going to come up with are not going to seduce you. At all." I'd watched myself dance in mirrors before and it wasn't pretty.

"I'm sure that's not true," Tuesday said, putting her hands on my hips. "All you need to do is move your hips. Come on, you can do it." I tried, but my whole bottom half moved, so I looked like I was a middle-aged dad trying to rock it out at a bowling alley after a few beers.

"No, isolate your hips. Like this." She moved until our hips were pressed together and I wasn't thinking about dancing. I could only feel the heat of her skin and the fact that there were only a few layers of fabric between us.

"Move with me," she said, her hands pushing my hips from one side to the other in a swaying motion as she did the same with her hips. The friction between us made me bite my lip so I didn't moan. This was the most erotic dancing lesson I'd ever had.

"There, you've got it," she said, but then I faltered and lost my rhythm.

"Sorry," I said, my face getting red. "I told you I wasn't a good dancer."

"That's okay," she said, digging her fingers into my hips. "I can think of something else you can do with your hips that I think you might like better." A whimpering sound emerged from my mouth and she smiled.

"Let's get you out of this outfit now."

Within moments I was naked, and I wasn't quite sure how it happened.

"Why am I always the first one naked? It's not fair," I whined.

"Because you're prettier," she said, as if that was a fact.

"Excuse me? Are you on drugs?" What in the hell was she talking about?

"You're prettier than me? That's not a secret, or a surprise," she said. That was not going to fly.

"There is one person here who is the prettiest, and it's not me," I said, tracing my fingers down her neck. She bit her bottom lip and shook her head.

"No way."

I leaned closer and whispered in her ear, "Yes way," before I took her earlobe between my teeth and bit it softly. A garbled sound came from her lips and I laughed. That was an end to that argument, for now.

"Now, let me take your clothes off," I said, placing a kiss on her neck.

"Uh huh," she said, and I loved that I'd rendered her as senseless as I got when she kissed my neck.

I got the shirt off, and wrestled a little with the bra, which was ridiculous because I took a bra off at least once a day. Hooking my fingers in the strings of the thong, I slid them down her legs. I helped her kick them aside and then ran my hands up and down the front of her thighs.

"You have the best thighs I've ever seen," I said.

"They're not too big?" she asked, muscles twitching.

"They're perfect." I kissed one thigh and then the other. "Let me show your thighs some appreciation." I drew her onto the bed and pushed her so she was on her back.

"When I first saw you, I couldn't stop thinking about how I wanted to lick each and every one of your muscles. I was too impatient to do that our first night, but I have plenty of patience now." I dragged my hand down the center of her chest and circled her belly button. She quivered in anticipation.

"I was going to start from the top and work my way down, but I don't think I'm going to do that." No, I was going to start from her feet.

Tuesday sat up, her face flushed.

"You don't have a foot fetish, do you?" I picked up her right foot and kissed the arch.

"Would it matter if I did?" She blew some hair out of her face.

"I mean, I'd have to get used to it. Not something I've had a whole lot of experience with." I smiled and kissed each one of her toes.

"No, I don't have a foot fetish, but it's good to know how you'd feel if I did." I kissed her heel, and then the top of her foot. Her ankle was next, then her unbelievable calf. I learned that she was ticklish behind her knees, a fact that I stored away for later use. Her knee had a tiny scar on it that I wanted to ask about later. I left her thigh for later and did the same routine to her other leg, stopping just short of her powerful thighs. Scooting forward, I situated myself between them. I had the perfect view of all her best physical attributes. Tuesday had pressed herself up on her elbows to watch me. Her pupils were large and her breathing erratic. I hadn't done much, but she was already having a hard time. Good. I wanted to drive her wild before making her come so hard, she'd never forget it, and then make her come at least two more times. I wanted to give her an unforgettable night.

Ignoring my own raging lust, I parted her thighs and licked my way upwards.

"I know your nipples are horribly neglected right now, but I will get to them, don't you worry." Oh, I'd get to them after round one.

Tuesday's skin was slightly salty and so warm, it was like her internal furnace was always on.

Curious, I softly bit one of her thighs and she bucked against me and made noises that said she'd enjoyed that. So I did it again, and again, leaving little red marks on her skin that faded too quickly for my liking. I wanted to leave marks on her. That was a new feeling.

Her front was lovely, but I had neglected her back and I needed to fix that.

"Can you roll over, babe?" The endearment came out of my mouth without me even intending to say it. I hoped she didn't notice that little slip. Tuesday flipped onto her stomach and turned her head to the side with a sigh.

I sat on my heels for a moment, just savoring the view of her ass and her back.

"This is the best view I've ever seen. Maybe tied with the front view of you. Then the Grand Canyon is second. The Eifel Tower is third." I scraped my nails down her back and circled one of her ass cheeks with a finger. I pinched it softly, wondering what would happen. She made a little surprised noise, but it wasn't one that told me not to do that again. I rubbed a circle on her skin and then gave her a quick little slap. Her hips jacked up and she let out an audible moan. No mistaking that.

"You like that?" I asked, landing another little spank on her ass.

She made a sound that I thought was a yes, and then arched her back and stuck her ass up higher, so I could reach it better. That was as good a sign as any, for sure.

"You keep surprising me, Tuesday Grímsdóttir." I punctuated every word with a spank and tested her limits by going pretty hard. I'd never really done this before, but the instinct came upon me naturally, and I was getting so turned on by her sounds and her movements and the increasing redness of her ass cheeks, I was ready to come just from that.

I landed a series of hard smacks on her ass, and she put her hand up and asked me to slow down.

"I'm sorry," I said, sitting back, horrified. I'd pushed her too far and now this was probably over. I was new to all this and didn't know what I was doing and I'd fucked it up. Typical.

"No, it's fine. You just found my limit and so did I. Now we know for next time." She rolled over on her front and winced a little.

"Is it weird that I hope I have marks?" she said.

"No, because I hope you do too," I admitted, and she smiled.

"Come here and kiss me." I propped myself on my arms and leaned down and ravished her mouth and let her work her magic with her teeth and her tongue. If the gym thing didn't work out, she could have a career as a professional kiss coach. I was sure someone had monetized that somewhere.

I straddled Tuesday's hips and rocked against them, and she pushed up to meet me and it took a little while before we were on the same rhythm, but we got to where it was working for both of us. Before the friction got to be too much, I snuck my hand between us and rubbed her clit. She gasped into my mouth and moaned.

"I know I said I was going to lick you all over, and I'm still planning on that, but I think you need to come first." She whimpered and shut her eyes, shoving her hips against my hand as I rocked it into her. Tuesday was so wet that one finger slid easily inside her, and then I added another after only a few thrusts. Moving from her mouth, I finally paid some attention to her boobs, playing and sucking on her nipples as I worked her lower down. Inner muscles clenched around my fingers and I knew she was close, so I increased the momentum, curling my fingers right where she needed them and she cried out, her hips shaking, her eyelids fluttering. I kept pumping my fingers until the pulses slowed and then stopped. Slowly, she opened her eyes and smiled at me, her chest glistening with perspiration.

"Holy fuck, I thought I was going to die. Turns out spanking is my thing," she said with a light laugh.

"Spanking is apparently my thing to, only being on the spanker end and not the spankee. Or maybe I like it? I don't know." Tuesday squinted at me.

"Do you want to find out?"

Chapter Fourteen

Turns out, spanking wasn't my thing. It just didn't do anything for me but feel annoying.

"It would probably be complicated if we both loved spanking. Then we'd have to hire someone to come and spank us simultaneously," she said. I shuddered at the thought.

"I'm definitely not fucking sharing you with anyone." Before now, I wouldn't have used the word "possessive" to describe myself, but I would claw anyone's eyes out who saw Tuesday like this right now.

"My vicious princess," she said, kissing my mouth. I'd made her come again, and she'd made me come twice, so we were even and had stopped for a break. Plus, the kittens were crying to be let in. I wrapped myself in a robe and went to open the door and let them waddle in.

"I'm sorry, mommy had to get laid," I said, picking them up and putting them on the bed. Tuesday was still completely naked under the blankets.

"Do you want to order something?" I asked. We'd already had dinner, but we needed to refuel, for sure.

"Yeah, I'm in the mood for sushi." As soon as she said it, I was too, so I ordered a bunch of rolls.

"One of us is going to have to put on clothes to go answer the door," I said, after I'd placed the order.

"Not it," Tuesday said, putting her finger on her nose. "Plus, it's your apartment." I growled at her.

"Fine. I'll get it. But only because you paid." That seemed fair enough. "But before I go get the food, you're going to come again." She threw back the blankets and pounced on me as I screamed. The babies were on the floor playing with some of our discarded clothes, so they didn't get squished in the mayhem.

"We have to put them out," I said. "It's too weird." Tuesday got up, completely naked, and put the kitties outside.

"I'm sorry!" she said, as she shut the door. "But mommy needs to get fucked." I waited for her on the bed as she stalked toward me. "It's time for me to pay you back for that first night." I couldn't think straight to remember what she was talking about.

Tuesday crawled on the bed and grabbed my ankles, flipping me over effortlessly. I looked at her over my shoulder and she put her hand under my belly and brought my hips up.

"Time for you to fuck *my* face." Before I knew what was happening, she'd widened my hips, propped a pillow under me and had set herself up right at my entrance. Her breath was hot on my thighs. Unsure of what to do, I waited.

"Come on, princess. Fuck my face." Never, in my entire life, had any sentence said in my presence been as sexy as that. I wished I could see her face, but that wasn't possible. I pushed myself back until I encountered something warm and wet.

"Ohhhhh," I moaned. That was good. That was *real* good. I moved my hips up and down and she made a little sound of pleasure, as if she was getting as much out of this as I was. I hoped she was.

I thrust a little harder, and she was there to meet me with her devious tongue, flicking my clit and licking me all up and down. I adjusted my hips and then, well, I fucked her face. She let me take the lead and do what I needed to do to bring myself to a shimmering orgasm that wrung the air from my lungs and every last drop of pleasure from my veins. After, I collapsed on the bed and couldn't turn myself over. My phone rang seconds later, and Tuesday answered it.

"The sushi is here, princess," she said.

"Uh huh." Those were the only two syllables I could get out. Tuesday chuckled and then left the room. I concentrated on trying to flip myself over onto my back. It took four tries before I succeeded. Tuesday walked in with the sushi seconds later.

"You doing okay there?" she asked.

"Yup," I said, sitting up. "Just a little wrung out." I was also tired as hell. The kitties followed Tuesday into the room, and I could tell they were mad and betrayed by us ignoring them.

"Come here, babies. I'm sorry." I gathered them onto the bed as Tuesday set out the sushi and handed me some chopsticks. The kittens went right for the sashimi, and I pushed one of the less expensive pieces toward them to share. They gobbled it up like greedy little beggars who hadn't been fed in years and then tried to go for more.

"This was a bad idea," I said, using my arm to block the kitties from getting to the precious sushi. Tuesday picked up the sushi and stood up.

"See, you don't have these issues with turtles," she pointed out, and I glared at her.

"Don't you dare talk about my precious babies that way.

Anyone but You

They are perfect." I covered myself with the blankets and then pulled the kittens into my lap.

"Do you want me to feed you? Is that what's going on?"

"It's the only way," I said in a dramatic voice. Tuesday rolled her eyes, but stayed standing and fed me a piece of sushi, and then took one for herself. We went back and forth like that until all of the rolls had been consumed and the kittens had fallen asleep again.

"I think we're safe now," I said, and Tuesday threw the empty containers in the trash, coming back to sit with me on the bed.

"Do you mind if I stay? I brought clothes just in case."

"Not only don't I mind if you stay, I very much want you to stay." The front door slammed and I heard the arrival of Zee. They never made a quiet entrance, ever.

"Zee's home. I want to go ask where they were, but also, I don't want to get out of bed or put clothes on." Not that it would matter. Zee and I had seen each other naked more times than we wanted to admit.

"Do you want to take a shower?" I asked. I was still pretty sweaty from all the sex.

"Are you sure it's okay if I stay?" Tuesday asked, and I just kissed her.

"I insist upon it."

~

IN FACT, Tuesday stayed longer than either of us planned. Sunday morning she woke up with me and we went out to find Zee cheerfully making us huevos rancheros. Tuesday was a little awkward at first, but Zee quickly broke the ice, and then I asked them where they'd been.

"Well, you got yourself a girlfriend, so I'm out there trying to get a boyfriend. I had a date." Their face was beaming, so it must have gone well.

"And?" I asked.

"We're going on a second date on Wednesday night." I squealed and hugged them, and then made them tell me all about the guy. I hoped Tuesday didn't feel left out, but she just ate her food and cooed at the kitties. So far, everything I heard about Zee's new man sounded great. They'd met through mutual friends and he'd moved recently to our neighborhood. He was a special ed teacher who also enjoyed rock climbing, knitting, and comics. I said that I wanted to meet him if they got further in their relationship. They told me that was a given, and I turned my attention back to Tuesday. She volunteered to help with the dishes and I wasn't going to stop her, so I let her load the dishwasher and clean the pans.

"You okay? I really felt like I had to catch up with Zee." She put her arms around me and kissed my forehead.

"It's fine. They're your best friend. I would never want to come between that, so stop worrying that I'm going to get mad or jealous. I'm not."

Okay, then. I took her word for it.

～

I DID HAVE to go to work, so Tuesday went home on Sunday to feed the turtles and change clothes.

"You're really diving in, aren't you?" Zee said, and I shook my head.

"I don't want to talk about it. I can't think about it." I didn't *want* to think about it, but now that she was gone, Tuesday was the only thing on my mind.

There were so many moments this weekend when we'd been laughing together, or she'd been talking to the kitties, or we'd been fucking when I had this feeling come over me so intense that it made me want to cry and laugh all at once. I wasn't going to put a label on that feeling because that would be saying that it was a real thing, and I wasn't ready for that.

It hadn't even been a week. I didn't like her. I certainly wasn't in—

No. I couldn't finish that thought. I wouldn't. It was impossible.

~

SUNDAY NIGHT SHE CAME BACK, even though I wasn't expecting her. She showed up on my doorstep with a bag and a sheepish look on her face.

"Didn't I see you earlier?" I said, stepping back to let her in after the shock had worn off. I'd just been trying to figure out what to do with myself tonight now that she wasn't here. I'd been planning on filing my nails and maybe listening to too many episodes of a podcast. Wild times.

"Yes, and I know I shouldn't be here, but it was boring at my apartment and the turtles told me to come." I burst out laughing.

"Oh, the turtles made you do it?"

She nodded solemnly.

"Yup. Blame the turtles."

I reached for her and we made out in the entry of my apartment while the kitties pawed at our legs for attention.

Zee made us dinner and we all ate together, like we'd been doing it for years. Tuesday took a bit to warm up, but she got there pretty fast with Zee. They had a way of doing that with people, which was why they were so good at their job.

Watching Zee make Tuesday laugh so hard that she wiped tears from her face made me have another one of those moments. It was like the space in my chest was too small for one organ in particular: my heart.

No. This wasn't happening. I coughed and then choked on some water. Tuesday patted me on the back.

"You okay?"

"Yup," I said, waving her off. "Fine. Completely fine."

I was not completely fine.

Later on, when we were on the couch and Tuesday played with my hair and sighed contentedly, I had another moment. Breathing became difficult and I had to calm myself. Again, Tuesday asked me if I was okay and I said I was.

Monday morning greeted me with another moment as I opened my eyes and found Tuesday awake and smiling at me with her puffy eyes and messy hair. I tried to swallow the feelings, tried to tell myself they weren't real, couldn't be real, but they screamed so loud that I couldn't drown them out, couldn't ignore them.

It simply wasn't possible to feel this way about her. Hell, a few days ago I didn't know if I *liked* her, and here I was, falling in—

Nope. Not going there again. I shook my head and kissed the tip of Tuesday's nose to distract me.

"We should probably get up," I said, my voice scratchy. "I have to get to work." She grinned and rolled on her back.

"*You* have to get to work. I don't have early classes today. I can stay in bed if I want." My eyes narrowed, and I leapt out of bed, yanking the covers off before she could do anything.

"Oh, you are asking for it," she said, jumping after me.

"No, no, stop!" I laughed and huddled in the corner with the blankets, but this was a losing battle.

"You can't win this, princess. Just give me the blankets." I clutched them even tighter.

"No," I said, and she shook her head.

"Then you asked for it." I screamed as she threw me over her shoulder and then back on the bed. I was mercilessly tickled until I begged for mercy.

"You're adorable when you beg, princess," she said.

"Why do you call me that?" I asked, when I was able to breathe again.

"Because I thought you were, at first. But now I call you that because it's cute and you're cute and I like it." That was fair. She hadn't commented on me calling her "babe" and I'd done it again a few times. I liked the way it felt to call her that.

"Why is your name Tuesday? And are you Icelandic? With that last name?" Tuesday sighed and lay next to me.

"What's with all the questions this morning?" I rolled onto my side.

"I don't know. Just things I've been wondering." It also distracted me from all the shit going on in my head. That swelling feeling hadn't left, and my heart was still too small for my chest.

"My parents thought I was going to be a boy, so they'd never picked out a girl's name. When I was born, my dad joked that they should just name me for the day of the week. So they did. Yes, he's from Iceland and my mother is half Spanish, half Japanese." I wanted to ask her more questions about her family, but if I did that, I was going to be late as fuck.

"You can interrogate me about my family later," she said through a yawn. "You'd better get going."

I kissed her hard before I left, and swallowed the words that wanted to come out of my mouth, but they stuck in my throat and bothered me all the way to the yoga studio. They bothered me while I called the poses for my first class and they bothered me while I talked to Ellen and Priya and finally reviewed applications for new teachers. It was time for me to hire at least one more, probably two more, teachers for the growing studio. I couldn't do it all on my own anymore.

Tuesday brought me lunch again, but I was busy giving someone a tour of the studio, so she left it on the front desk for me before she went back downstairs. I didn't have CrossFit tonight, but about ten minutes before the last class of the night, she came up the stairs, a brand-new yoga mat rolled on her shoulder.

"Excuse me, I'd like to buy a membership," she said, taking the mat down and grinning at me.

"Would you now?" I asked, ignoring the flutters that threatened to overwhelm me at the sight of her. It had only been a few hours and I wanted to throw myself at her as if we'd been parted for years.

"Yes, I would. I want to take classes from the best yoga teacher in town." A crowd of people came in behind her, a bunch of friends from the bank down the street who were all coming to class tonight. She stepped aside as I checked everyone in, and then got my attention.

"What?" I said.

"I forgot something," she said, and leaned over the desk so she was right there. "I'm ready to kiss you in public." Then she did, putting her lips on my surprised mouth. The sounds of woops and cheers greeted my ears and I pulled back, wobbling a little on my feet.

"Go Sutton," Jenna, one of my regular clients, said. "You get it.!"

My face went red and Tuesday winked.

"I'm going to go set up my mat." She left me there, unsteady on my feet and with a lot of people asking a lot of questions. Oh, I was going to get her.

Anyone but You

I MADE it through class without kissing her, or doing anything else. I got into teacher mode, and only a few times remembered that Tuesday was in the room. Good thing to know I could keep my integrity even when she was there.

Tuesday was the last one in the room, and I walked over as she lounged on her mat with a contented smile on her face.

"You know, I think this yoga has helped my lifting." I sat down next to her.

"I can't believe you kissed me in front of everyone. Now I'm going to have to field all kinds of questions and I'm never going to hear the end of it." She blinked at me in surprise.

"I thought that was what you wanted. Not to be a secret. And we did say a week. Okay, so it wasn't exactly a full week, but still. I was ready to kiss you and to tell people that we're together."

She was right, and I was overreacting, but I had a storm brewing inside and it was throwing me into turmoil.

"I have a problem, Tuesday. A big problem." Her eyebrows pulled together in concern and she reached for me.

"What is it?"

I took a deep breath and let it out.

"I like you. A lot."

She laughed. Tuesday actually threw her head back and laughed.

"Of course you like me. That's obvious. You don't spend entire weekends with people you don't like, if you don't have to. You definitely like me." I hated how smug she was being about this, so I said something that was sure to silence her.

"Oh, yeah? If you thought that was obvious, then try this: I love you!" My declaration was greeted with silence.

"What?" she said, shaking her head as if she hadn't heard me clearly. "You love me? Are you fucking serious?"

"Yes, I love you, Tuesday. I do."

Yes, I was. I had never been more serious in my life. I hadn't wanted to put a name to that feeling I'd been having for the past few days, because it didn't seem possible, but there was no other word for it: love. I'd gone right from not being sure if I liked her to being so in love with her that I couldn't even breathe.

Tuesday nodded and breathed, pulling at the edge of the yoga mat. I waited for her to speak. To tell me that I was out of my mind. To tell me that I couldn't love her, it was just lust. I waited for her to tell me I was ridiculous. I waited for her to run out of the room and never speak to me again. She lifted those unbelievable blue eyes and spoke, at last.

"You love me? Well, that's good, because I love you too."

If I hadn't been sitting, I would have fallen over.

"You love me?" I asked. This couldn't be happening. None of this was real. I pressed my hands to the floor to ground me.

"Yes, I love you. I wanted to ignore it, and I honestly don't know how this happened, but I do. So I guess that means I like you too." I tried to swallow and failed.

"You love me and I love you and you like me and I like you, did I get that right?" I said, and she nodded. "What the hell do we do now?" Tuesday dusted off her hands and stood up, holding her hands out to me.

"We kiss?"

Oh. That seemed like a good idea. Kissing was definitely the right thing.

Before her lips met mine, she smiled and touched her forehead to mine.

"I can't believe I love you. And I like you. How could I let that happen? I don't fall in love with people like this. And not in less than a week. What am I doing?" she questioned, and I had been thinking just about the same thing.

"I don't know. Everyone is going to say that it's too fast and that it's not real." Tuesday laughed and I stroked my hands up and down her sides.

"It is too fast, but it's definitely real. I wouldn't be willing to take a risk like this if it wasn't. I was ready to not date for years, and I might have moments where I get a little scared. It's not even loving you that scares me, it's trusting another person not to fuck me over again." I kissed the tip of her nose and then her forehead.

"I'm just going to fuck you. No over required," I said, because those were the first words that came out of my mouth. Tuesday laughed.

"That's good to know. There are no guarantees that this is going to work out, and the fact that I'm your landlord is a little sticky." I hadn't even thought about that factor.

"You can't fuck me over either," I said. Tuesday nodded.

"Okay."

It wasn't going to be as easy as that; it never was. There were no guarantees that we wouldn't have a brutal breakup, but I didn't want to worry or think about that right now. I only wanted to make out with my girlfriend, Tuesday, who I loved and liked.

"Let's kiss instead of talking. We're always better at the kissing." Tuesday smoothed my hair from my face.

"I can't believe I love you," she said, but it was with a tone of wonder. Instead of answering, I kissed her instead.

∽

WE KISSED and she had to be the one to put a stop to it and remind me that we both needed to lock up for the night and go home and not make out on her sweaty yoga mat instead.

"Which home are we going to?" I asked. I hoped she would say that she wanted to go to her place. I was hankering to sleep in that big bed after being crowded with her in my smaller bed. After sleeping multiple nights with her, I had learned one thing above all: Tuesday took up a lot of room when she slept. Every single one of her limbs reached for a different corner, and she sprawled out as if she didn't have a care in the world. No wonder she needed a big bed.

"My place? Unless you want to go to yours. I don't know if my back wants to sleep another night on your mattress, though." She winced.

"Hey now, that mattress has served me well since college, don't diss my mattress." Tuesday gave me a look.

"Princess, if you've had your mattress since college, it might be time for a new one." I didn't want to admit that she had a point, so I just kissed her neck instead.

"Hey, now, you can't distract me with ohhhhh." She moaned as I found the right spot to suck that made her incoherent.

"Haha, I win," I said, giving the spot one last little kiss. "It's fine, we can go to your place." I would miss the babies, but they'd have to get used to me being gone more. Zee was with them when I wasn't, and when Zee had their dates, Tuesday and I would go to my place. It would be fine.

"I think I should make us a really good dinner. How does roast chicken with potatoes and Brussels sprouts sound?" My mouth instantly started to water.

"It sounds incredible. I'm so blessed with people in my life who are good at cooking. I'll never learn at this rate." I probably should, though. Just in case. I couldn't be an adult who didn't know how to fry an egg.

"I can teach you. We can start slow, but I don't mind teaching you." She didn't know how wonderful that was. My parents had tried to teach me when I was a kid and instantly became frustrated when I'd get distracted by something else, or put the burner on the wrong setting, or forget ingredients moments after reading the recipe. Something told me Tuesday would have more patience with me. I was looking forward to that.

There were so many things to look forward to. Tuesday doing more yoga. Me (reluctantly) doing more CrossFit. More dares. More kissing. More turtle raves and kitten dance parties. More hanging out with Zee and watching them become friends with Tuesday. More sex. So much more sex. More of everything.

More complications, definitely, but I couldn't be completely focused on those. Right now I wanted to bask in the happy, and that looked like going to Tuesday's apartment and watching her as she made the best roast chicken I'd ever tasted in my entire life.

∽

"HOW DID WE LET THIS HAPPEN?" she asked later, as we lay in her bed after fucking each other slowly and softly. There was a time and a place for a hard fuck, but tonight it hadn't felt right.

"Do you mean the sex? You took my clothes off. That's what happened." I still hadn't managed to get Tuesday naked before I was naked, but I wasn't going to stop trying.

"No, I mean falling in love. I was not ready for this, I wasn't looking for this, and I definitely didn't want it. I tried, but I guess I didn't fight too hard, because here we are." She kissed the side of my forehead.

"I wasn't looking for this either. And I realize now that I've never really been in love. Not like this. Sure, I said the words, and I did have strong feelings, but this is . . . this is everything." I rolled onto my stomach so I could stare at her gorgeous face.

"We still don't know that much about each other and we might want to fix that."

"Okay, princess, what do you want to know?" I asked her tons of questions, like who her favorite teacher was, and what was the most embarrassing thing that had ever happened to her, and when the first time she had sex was, and what her ten-year plan was. I answered after she asked me and it was good and probably one of the longest conversations we'd had so far. Strange that I'd fallen in love with her not knowing so many things, but love wasn't like a job interview. You didn't get all the facts and history and check references before you fell.

I did like her, and I'd been ridiculous to deny that. Sure, she *had* been an asshole when we'd first met, but now that I understood her better, I realized that the assholery was a symptom of the extreme stress and trauma she'd been under. Sure, that didn't absolve her completely, but she told me that after she'd been such a jerk to me in those first few weeks, she'd started seeing a therapist about getting over her breakup, and for help dealing with her parent's deaths. Tuesday was much more willing to talk about them now, which made me feel so good that she trusted me so much with something so painful.

Tuesday had been really close with her parents, especially her dad. She'd wanted to be a dentist, like him, but had gotten into fitness in college instead.

"He seemed shocked that I wanted to go into dentistry when I told him it wasn't my passion after all. I guess I just assumed that was what he wanted me to do, but he told me he just wanted me to be happy. He really was amazing." She showed me some pictures of him and her mom, smiling on the top of a mountain, and waving from a cruise ship.

"They did everything together, always going on adventures around the world. And they loved each other, so much." I wiped some tears from her cheeks.

"Thank you so much for sharing them with me." I kissed both of her salty cheeks and held her close.

"Thank you for listening," she whispered.

We fell asleep in each other's arms that night, and the next morning I woke up and realized I'd fallen even deeper in love with her. If this trend continued, I was going to be more in love with her every day and I didn't know how much love I could handle.

"What are you thinking about?" she asked in a scratchy voice.

"How much I love you," I said. "It scares me, honestly."

She stroked my face and smiled.

"That's how you know it's love."

∼

"LET ME GET THIS RIGHT: You are in love with Tuesday," Zee said as they carefully poached some eggs the next morning.

"Yes. I know, I know. I don't need a lecture, or for you to tell me it's too fast, or whatever advice you want to give me. All I want is for you to be happy for me." Zee opened their mouth and then closed it. They fished two perfectly poached eggs out of the water and lay them on a paper towel before turning to give me their full attention.

"I could say so many things right now, but the one thing I'm going to say is this: I'm happy for you and I think you two are great together." They held out their arms and gave me a hug and I almost started to cry. Having them say that and mean it was so important. It had been the two of us against the world for so long and there was no one whose opinion I valued more than Zee.

"I love you so much," I said, choking back tears.

"I love you too," Zee said, their voice thick with emotion. "I'll always support you, no matter what."

"Same," I said, and pulled back from the hug, grabbing a paper towel to blow my nose with. They grabbed one too and then we both started laughing.

"Now tell me about this boyfriend of yours." They rolled their eyes.

"He's not my boyfriend yet. We haven't even been on a second date."

"But you totally like him, like him, don't you?" I said, dancing around them. Their face got red and they blew their hair out of their eyes and went back to the eggs.

"I'm ignoring what's happening right now."

"But you likeeeeee him," I sang.

"Shut up," they said, but their face kept getting redder. I cackled in victory.

"You're in love, so hush."

"Yeah, I am." I let out a contented sigh. I was utterly and completely in love with Tuesday Grímsdóttir. My lady, my love, my landlord. Maybe my rent would go down?

Epilogue

A FEW WEEKS later I was in the yoga studio, messing around with a yoga flow with Tuesday. She'd made remarkable improvement in yoga in such a short time that I was almost mad about it.

"You can't be better at yoga than me," I said, as she did a flawless side crow.

"That's not the point of yoga," she said, flowing back into downward-facing dog.

"Yeah, yeah, I know. But you can't be better at CrossFit *and* yoga. It's not allowed." Tuesday jumped her feet forward and stood all the way up, and stuck her tongue out at me.

"You're getting better. Your pull-ups are really coming along. In no time you're going to be doing butterfly pull-ups." I highly doubted that because I wasn't a fucking gymnast, but I'd give it a try. I'd survived the Fundamentals class and had officially gotten myself a membership. I worked out twice a week now, in addition to yoga, but I was probably going to go up to three times a week once my new yoga teacher, Anne, started. I was also interviewing a part-time front desk person to handle check in so I could focus more on running the business. It was past time, and Tuesday had even hinted that she knew of a few places where I could expand, but I wasn't ready for that yet. Too much change in too short a time already.

Tuesday was killing it with the gym. She'd come up with all kinds of innovative promotions and had hired a rockstar social media person and I was a little jealous, not going to lie. She'd agreed that we could partner for some promotions, so I was fully intending on grabbing some of her customers and bringing them in to yoga, and I was also going to send some of my yoga students downstairs for CrossFit.

Zee and Tuesday had fallen into an easy friendship, and they even hung out sometimes without me, which made me a teeny bit jealous, but I didn't tell either of them that. I'd also introduced Tuesday to the rest of my friends and they all warmed up to her quickly. She could be totally personable when she wanted to be, but she was still hot and mean sometimes. At least now I understood why, and I didn't take it too seriously.

Yes, she did play her music too loud, and her packages did get delivered upstairs, and she had a tendency to shut down emotionally when she was upset. We were still trying to figure each other out, but it was worth it. She was worth it. Plus, I wasn't a perfect person and had plenty of my own flaws that she knew about, and some she was just discovering.

I hoped I was worth it.

"You ready to go?" Tuesday asked, cleaning her mat and then rolling it up. Tonight we were going to my place because Zee had a date with their new boyfriend, Chris. I'd met him and he was a total sweetheart, and Zee was completely smitten. I'd never seen them so into a guy before, so I teased them endlessly about it. They got me back for being in love with Tuesday, so we broke even.

"Yeah, let's go. What are we making tonight?" Tuesday

had taken on the task of teaching me basic cooking skills. It wasn't going well so far, but she had endless patience for my mistakes.

"Fried chicken with macaroni and cheese and collard greens." My eyes went wide. That sounded like a lot, and I didn't want to mess that much food up. Tuesday must have seen the panic in my eyes because she put her hands on my shoulders.

"Breathe. It will be fine. You've got this. I'll be right there with you. And it doesn't matter if it doesn't taste good, or you burn it. I'll eat it anyway." That was true. Tuesday was not picky about food. She'd eat just about anything.

"Okay," I said, and we locked up together before heading down to her car. Since we spent most of our nights together now, it didn't make sense to take two cars everywhere.

"We just have to stop and get a few things," Tuesday said, and we went to the grocery store together. She thought nothing of pushing the cart with one hand and holding my hand with the other. Sometimes I still had to remind myself that this was real, and we were together. So surreal.

Tuesday grabbed pasta, cheese, hot sauce, and a few other things. I just followed as she did her thing.

"You should probably teach me how to grocery shop too," I said, and she gave me a look.

"You don't know how to grocery shop?"

"I mean, I do. I've done it, but I always feel like I'm all over the place and I put a bunch of things in my cart, and then I have nothing to make meals out of when I get home. Also, Zee does most of the shopping since they actually do the cooking." It had been years since I'd stocked the fridge or the pantry on my own.

"Oh, you precious princess," she said, pulling the back of my hand up to kiss it. "I'll teach you how to grocery shop. Not tonight, but we can do that this weekend. As long as you do one thing for me return."

"What's that?" I asked. She looked around before leaning in and whispering in my ear.

"Spank me and then fuck me senseless." I gasped and heat flooded my body.

"Fuck the fried chicken, let's do that now." I grabbed the cart and started racing down the aisle, Tuesday following behind me and laughing.

"I'm starving, so maybe we can do dinner first?" she asked, when she caught up with me at the checkout.

"Fine, but think about how good that food would taste after," I said.

Tuesday sighed.

"Do you want to just order in and then we can make this another night?" There was an idea. I pulled her in for a kiss.

"That is the best idea you've had all day, babe," I said. The word rolled off my tongue with no problem now, and I knew she liked it, so I made use of that word whenever I could.

"No, the best idea I've had was annoying the shit out of you so you'd come downstairs and catch me working out," she said with a smirk.

"Wait, you did that on *purpose*?" Why hadn't that occurred to me?

"I wanted to get your attention," she said with a shrug, loading up the conveyor belt.

"You are shameless," I said, shaking my head. "You could have just told me you thought I was cute."

"I could have, but annoying you was way more fun." I sputtered and then she kissed me until I forgot what I was supposed to be mad about.

"Sorry not sorry, princess."

Like this book? Reviews are SO appreciated! They can be long or short, or even just a star rating. Thank you so much!

Looking for another city romance? Try Didn't Stay in Vegas!

Sign up for my newsletter for access to free books, sales, and up-to-date news on new releases!

Acknowledgments

I'm so proud of this book. I know I should say that about all my books, but whatever. I'm EXTRA proud of this one, and I have a few people to thank:

Firstly, always, to my editor, Laura, who kills it every time and learned all about yoga terms and the proper formatting for them, and who adds little notes and comments to every book that make me laugh and keep me going when I'm editing. I wouldn't be the writer I am without you.

Second, to everyone who helped with the cover reveal, and who was SO enthusiastic about lady abs. I knew that dude abs sold books, so I decided "why not?" when it comes to lady abs. I guess y'all like that, huh?

Third, to my Patreon supporters, Brandi and Elly, you are incredible and I am so lucky to have you supporting me. I couldn't do this without you, and to all my other Patreon supporters, you have no idea what it means to me. Thank you.

Fourth, and not least, to my love. Thanks for helping me with CrossFit knowledge and for putting up with me attaching myself to my computer for days and not paying attention to you. You're my rock, my heart, my everything.

About the Author

Chelsea M. Cameron is a New York Times/USA Today Best Selling author from Maine who now lives and works in Boston. She's a red velvet cake enthusiast, obsessive tea drinker, vegetarian, former cheerleader and world's worst video gamer. When not writing, she enjoys watching infomercials, singing in the car, tweeting (this one time, she was tweeted by Neil Gaiman) and playing fetch with her cat, Sassenach. She has a degree in journalism from the University of Maine, Orono that she promptly abandoned to write about the people in her own head. More often than not, these people turn out to be just as weird as she is. Connect with her on Twitter, Facebook, Instagram, Bookbub, Goodreads, and her Website. If you liked this book, please take a few moments to **leave a review**. Authors really appreciate this and it helps new readers find books they might enjoy. Thank you!

Other books by Chelsea M. Cameron:

The Noctalis Chronicles

Fall and Rise Series

My Favorite Mistake Series

The Surrender Saga

Rules of Love Series

UnWritten

Behind Your Back Series

OTP Series

Brooks (The Benson Brothers)

The Violet Hill Series

Unveiled Attraction

Anyone but You

Didn't Stay in Vegas

Wicked Sweet

Christmas Inn Maine

Bring Her On

The Girl Next Door

Who We Could Be

Castleton Hearts

Anyone but You is a work of fiction. Names, characters, places and incidents are either the product of the author's imagination or are use fictitiously. Any resemblance to actual persons, living or dead, events, business establishments or locales is entirely coincidental.

No part of this book may be reproduced, scanned or distributed in any printed or electronic form without permission. All rights reserved.

Copyright © 2019 Chelsea M. Cameron

Editing by Laura Helseth

Cover by Alessandra Morgan and Chelsea M. Cameron

Printed in Great Britain
by Amazon